# The Gecko Tribe
## Serpent of Fire

by Michael Harries

To Katie.

Enjoy the adventure.

Regards

Michael Harries

# THE GECKO TRIBE

## SERPENT OF FIRE

# Michael Harries

First Published in 2004 by Gecko Adventures

National Library of Australia Cataloguing-in-Publication Data:
Harries, Michael 1968 –
The Gecko Tribe: Serpent of Fire

ISBN 097568590-2

1. Geckos – juvenile fiction. 2. Anaconda- Juvenile fiction. 2. Bolivia – Juvenile fiction. I. Title.

A823.4

The Gecko Tribe – Serpent of Fire

Cover by Matt Torode www.tincup.tv
Author Photo by Michael Harries
Typeset by Jaime Lee at Breakout Design in Stempel Garamon Roman 11pt
Produced by Gecko Adventures

Disclaimer
All contact details given in this book were current at the time of publication, but are subject
to change. All care has been taken in the preparation of the information herein, but no
responsibility can be accepted by the publisher or author for any damages resulting from
the misinterpretation of the work.

# TABLE OF CONTENTS

## ABOUT THE AUTHOR

Michael Harries was born in Sydney and his basic philosophy is that 'life is a journey, not a destination'. The "GECKO TRIBE - SERPENT OF FIRE" is his first adventure novel.

Michael's fascination for adventure travel led him throughout South America, Africa, the Middle East, North America, Europe and Asia. As a teacher Michael decided to write THE GECKO TRIBE to educate, excite and encourage learning.

An intrigue and degree in geography has allowed Michael to focus on the South American continent where the dynamic landscapes are brought to life in this, the first of THE GECKO TRIBE books.

## ACKNOWLEDGEMENTS

I would like to thank Charlotte for her encouragement and belief in me. To Matt Torode, your creativity and designs have been amazing. To my family and friends – thanks for your support. To my mother and father, it has been a tough year in 2004; I love you very much and am excited that we all get to see this book published.

# DEDICATION

To Jessica, Sam and Ben.
I hope your lives are full of adventure and imagination.

# 1. The Gecko Tribe of Sydney

He stood frozen against the metal pillar as the feverish attacks continued. The eroded sheet of metal above his head was the only protection against the piercing weapons of his enemies.

"WHACK, WHACK!" came the ear jarring thuds as his mortal enemies edged closer and closer to his slightly hidden body.

The metal barrier would not last as it crumpled and twisted with each blow from their beaks.

Jet's large beady eyes scanned the surrounding area looking for opportunity and escape. As he scanned the area his small padded paw slipped on the metal surface and became an offering to the relentless seagulls.

"AWWKKK" cried the larger of the two seagulls as it grasped Jet's leg.

The pain was intense and tears formed in the corner of his eyes. This was it, Jet had to either counter attack or be the dinner for these two scavenger birds.

Jet leapt from his hidden cavity performing a mid air roll that he hoped would free his painful limb from the seagull's mouth. The seagull's head twisted as the weight of the small gecko ripped against it's beak. Jet's body was released and he plummeted two metres onto yet another metal girder that made up the bridge's gigantic framework.

The seagulls darted from their perches fearing their small meal was escaping.

Jet eyed the girder below with suction cup paws at the ready. He landed relatively flat but his wounded leg buckled under his weight. The two seagulls swooped above Jet's body but he managed to duck and weave from their snapping beaks.

He needed some extra luck and it was fast running out. Some electrical cable angled down a beam just next to his body. He looped his three healthy paws over the wire and slid into the cavity below. The seagulls could not follow and Jet had once again escaped by the narrowest of margins. They squawked loudly as he disappeared from their gaze.

Jet rested momentarily and breathed a large sigh of relief. *"What am I doing,"* he thought to himself as he summed up his self destructive mode. He rested a few moments more but was jolted back into reality with the realisation that he may miss the morning roll call again. He had been warned before by the colony leaders and would be severely punished if he was late again. He hobbled as fast as he could along the interconnecting grey girders of the giant bridge.

She could not believe Jet was running late. Mala steadied the nerves in her emerald tail. A sudden twitch would alert the assembly to the empty place beside her in the row. Ahead, along the steel girder, rows of stiff-backed geckos waited in position for the roll call. Very slowly she moved her head. If she turned ever so slightly, her enormous left eye could look to the rear without attracting too much attention. The last three rows were filing into place. *Where was he?*

Mala couldn't believe he'd gone again. The bridge dwellers never left the Harbour Bridge. That was the rule. No gecko ever broke it, or so they were told.

A flicker of vibration in the girder below alerted Mala. It was Jet! His mottled red body appeared like magic through a rust hole in the steel at her feet. He winked up cheekily at his friend and then whipped into place just as his name was called. The pain in his leg was hidden from others.

Jet and Mala lived in a gecko colony on the Sydney Harbour Bridge. The colony was situated where the large metal girders connected to the sandstone pylon on the northern arm of the bridge. The myriad of small crevasses provided shelter and protection for the colony, which numbered more than one hundred nocturnal reptiles.

Jet was a young male who had recently begun as a junior in the Lookout Guards. The Lookout Guards were the protective and military force that dominated the gecko colony. They were governed by the unsympathetic leader General Vorax. Everyone had to work in the colony for the well-being of it's existence, and for Jet, being in the Lookout Guards was the only job that was likely to capture his attention for any period of time.

Jet was assigned to Levis, an elderly gecko that had chronic arthritis. Levis's condition forced their duties to be confined to the lower harbour pylon away from the action. Jet's desire was to be a Pinnacle Guard, located at the very spire of the towers. However, the hierarchy of the colony and Jet's inexperience forced him to a lesser position. The young gecko and his ailing mentor were situated close to the dormitories and egg hatchery on the northern pylon.

That night they huddled in a sandstone crack to escape the beating wind and rain.

"Reckon there won't be many gulls about tonight," observed Levis.

The gulls were the worst enemy of the geckos and they were responsible for the disappearance of some careless colony members. Being small and fragile creatures, the geckos were very vulnerable.

"When it's clear and calm, that's when we have to be especially cautious of those carnivorous birds," added Levis.

Jet sighed. If only Levis knew what he had been through already today he would not even mention the gulls. Jet sat back and pondered the existence of the colony whose lives revolved around protecting themselves from harm and never being able to live life to the fullest. A life without excitement – he needed more.

As Jet's cold-blooded body lost some warmth he dozed off slightly, but was sprung to life when prodded in the ribs by Tokay, the watch foreman. Tokay, a burly looking gecko had arrived unexpectedly, as was his habit. He liked to surprise his troops to check their vigilance. It was easy to see from his unusual size and brisk manner why he was in charge. Rumour had it that he had once fought off twenty seagulls in his time and that a toe on his right foot was eaten by one of the birds. Tokay was hardened and difficult to communicate with, but was very good in the position he held. He was the code expert of the colony and had invented all the different calling codes for communication between each of the lookouts. Jet respected Tokay's talents and in his street-smart manner, he had learned to recognise and make the secret clicking noises during his training. However, Jet and Tokay never really bonded as individuals. Tokay's serious attitude conflicted heavily with Jet's larrikin antics. More than once Jet had been in trouble for his practical jokes and overly adventurous nature. Tokay was always watching him.

Tokay had brought some insects to share for their dinner. The onshore winds that channelled down the Sydney Harbour supplied a diversity of food across the bridge for the geckos to devour. Jet finished his portion and Tokay dismissed him.

"Have yourself a break. I just want to have a quick word to Levis here," he ordered.

Jet hobbled off into the maze of cracks within the pylon wall trying to hide his sore leg. His body was minute compared to the massive structural components of the bridge. His cold legs warmed up as he moved, but his time out on the exposed beams was shortened by the freezing wind and rain which quickly cooled his cold blood even further. Jet returned to his post fifteen minutes later and arrived unnoticed by Tokay and Levis who continued speaking in low tones.

"Hemi said you would remember," whispered Tokay.

"Oh I remember a'right. Though I'd never let on to Hemi or any of the General's Henchmen," replied Levis.

"They're not henchmen, they're just doing their job Levis, like the rest of us," argued Tokay.

"They're 'enchmen all right, them chief guards, I seen what they did to the one they brought back 'ere," retorted Levis.

"Hemi said none of the deserters had survived."

"None after they pushed Nephrusus off the bridge."

"That's not what I've been told!"

"They only tell you what they want you to know Tokay. Believe an old gecko that was there at the time rather than the propaganda *they* tell you."

Tokay opened his mouth to respond but stopped as he noticed Jet out of the corner of his eye. His face tightened as he stared at Jet. Jet was not meant to overhear this conversation.

"Fairly cold out there, I hope you've got a warmer sentry spot for me tomorrow night," Jet babbled his words.

Tokay's long tongue cleaned his eyes suspiciously. The big gecko nodded curtly and was gone without even saying farewell.

"Ow much did ya 'ear?" Levis asked.

"I don't know what you mean," replied Jet, attempting to look wide-eyed.

"Ya sure as well do, ya little skink! Don't think 'cause I'm old in me bones that me brain 'as gone too. Now tell me what ya 'eard or I'll hang ya over the edge by your dangly tail!" Levis roared.

Jet stared into the intensity of Levis's eyes but said nothing.

Levis shrugged and changed his tone. His persona softened and his eyes shone deeply from beneath his wrinkled old face. "What did you hear Jet?"

Jet told Levis what he had overheard and this concerned Levis.

"Please don't tell Tokay what I heard," begged Jet.

"Y' think I'm that stupid? He'd report the both of us. He shouldn't be asking about those incidents anyway. They happened before 'is time." Levis paused in silence. "Some of the gecko rebels got punished and one escaped the bridge, but I couldn't tell him that. If I do, he may try to reopen the case. I don't want that."

A low foghorn sounded from the bitterly cold harbour below.

"Who got away?" Jet asked.

Levis was silent then looked thoughtfully at Jet. "I can't tell you lad… but I think you know."

Jet eyes glazed over as his thoughts deepened.

"No more questions," finished Levis. "It's better if you don't know what 'appened – you're safer that way."

Jet was silent, but the curiosity burned to the very tips of his suction capped toes.

In the following weeks Levis pretended nothing had been said. Tokay visited them less and less often but when he did they could tell there was caution in his attitude.

Life continued in the colony. The geckos that were old enough went about their assigned work from dusk until first light. At first light the colony came together for roll call where General Vorax made the same repetitive authoritative speeches.

"The bridge is a dangerous place and we must unite as one to keep our existence. I know this is harsh and you sometimes feel confined but it is for the sake of the colony. Our rules and punishments are for the good of you all," he would bellow in his monotone voice. Then the geckos were escorted to their dormitories. No one stayed in the light. No one complained. No one questioned. No one ever left the bridge.

All appeared to be mundane and in order until an emergency meeting of the guards was called after sunrise. This was very peculiar and Jet's innate curiosity led his actions. All the chief guards were beginning to congregate as dawn broke over Sydney. Jet pretended to sleep in his dormitory until the others were silent. He then crawled up the wall and onto the ceiling of the dormitory and scurried upside down to the doorway. In this manner he would avoid detection if the guards returned suddenly. He didn't have a plan. He turned left. Using the suction pads on his feet he quickly navigated the passageways, past the egg hatchery and arachnid food storage, to the rear of the elder's dormitory.

Here he stopped dead in his tracks. Voices, low and secret, were floating out through the small air vent. Jet recognised the grave voice of Levis talking to the Chief Guards. He had been summoned before them and was talking about......... Jet.

"So like 'is father," said Levis.

"But you mustn't give him any ideas," warned an aggressive voice. "It could be a disaster for the entire colony. You remember what it was like for the rest of us when Sam left."

"I told him that it was better he does not know the truth but he keeps asking.... his curiosity is insatiable," Levis replied.

As Jet listened, totally captivated, the story unfolded. Years before, Jet's father Sam had claimed to have found evidence of a master colony in a time before the Gecko's lived on the Bridge, a time before the Generals, a time of freedom. Together with a small band of adventurers Sam had planned a journey to trace their ancestry, to find the beginning of gecko heritage, a Holy Grail, so to speak. But at the last minute the plan was foiled when one of the team members, Geera, had been caught storing insects for their travel rations. The chief guards had dragged him away for questioning. Under threat of torture Geera had revealed the entire plan but refused to name the others. Geera was tried for treason and placed in the solitary confinement of a gecko prison for a period of one year.

When Jet's father Sam and the third member, Nephrusus, got word of their friend's imprisonment they said goodbye to their wives and escaped that night. However, Nephrusus never reached the rendezvous point. The additional patrols had picked him up at the northern approach to the pylon. Sam had vanished.

Jet listened to the Chief Guard's conversation long into the daybreak. He crouched uncomfortably, silently listening to every syllable spoken by the concerned geckos. In his head the thoughts of adventure spun a mystical longing deep inside. He crept into bed just as the sun was at it's peak in the sky.

Mala awoke as Jet crawled past her.

"Your curiosity will be your downfall," she whispered.

*She was very concerned about him.*

# 2. The Prison

On patrol that night Jet began asking Levis random questions until he honed in on the topic of interest. Jet wanted to know if Geera was still in prison.

"Where is the prison located Levis?" Jet queried.

"Why?" came a quick and defensive reply.

"Just interested. We hear about it but nobody knows where it is. I was just wondering if it was a rumour that the generals use as a scare tactic to keep us all obedient."

"The secrecy is for safety reasons. The generals believe that the inmates may have a bad influence on the colony and so we built it far away at the base of the north pylon."

"You helped build it?"

"Yes. I haven't been there since. Nor do I want to go." Levis should not have said so much.

"It's of no concern to us," Levis warned.

"I agree," Jet replied, but his eyes told a different story.

Jet decided he would visit the prison.

Whenever you want time to speed up, it never does. Jet anxiously waited for the sunrise as he needed to confront Mala with his new found information.

During the morning roll call Jet was fidgety.

He tapped Mala on the leg then whispered out of the corner of his wide mouth, "I need your help."

Mala took a deep breath. What was he up to now she pondered? She reflected on the tension that Jet brought to her life. He was always in some form of trouble, but at least he made life interesting, she grinned to herself.

Once roll call had finished Jet and Mala were escorted back to the adolescent's dormitory.

Jet walked beside her and revealed his plan.

Mala's eyes widened with every word. She was hesitant but excited.

"Are you sure you know what you're doing?"

"Not really," he shrugged and smiled wickedly, "but I do know there is more to life than this place. My Dad's out there somewhere and I think he is still alive."

"You mean Sam is still alive?" Mala was astonished.

"I believe he is and I want to find him," Jet stated.

Mala's intelligent eyes shone deeply and her shimmering emerald body reflected the morning light. She felt reluctant but knew Jet would get into trouble if he attempted this alone.

"OK. I will go with you but on one condition."

"Anything!"

"We use our heads not our egos. You listen to me when I sense danger."

"You got it!"

Mala was unsure whether Jet had agreed just to placate her. She knew "danger" was Jet's middle name.

"I don't want to go to prison Jet. They have targeted me for the Intelligence Patrol and I am starting to read human language," Mala smiled proudly.

"I swear on my life. You won't get into trouble," Jet promised.

"That's what I am afraid of," Mala laughed.

"We'll leave today while everyone sleeps," Jet whispered with excitement.

An hour went by before the adolescent ward drifted off to sleep. The sun was now well into the sky and the colony was silent. Jet made a faint birdcall to indicate his movement and Mala followed him silently out through the doorway.

"Let's go," he whispered.

Mala was not convinced but Jet's lively personality and adventurous spirit certainly entertained and excited her.

They crept stealthily along the grey metal girders to the boundary of the colony region. Approximately one hundred geckos lived in this colony, but as these geckos were only fifteen centimetres long, the combined living area was small. The food storage, sleeping areas and community living were spread between the girders that connected into the northern pylon. These areas had to be minimal in order to escape human attention.

Jet and Mala now looked vertically down the large sandstone face to the base where Levis had said the prison was located. The south and north pylons, while structurally insignificant to the bridge, rose over seventy metres from the water's edge. Mala and Jet only had to descend the lower forty metres from the colony level.

Jet began the descent head first as he cautiously manoeuvred over the sandstone blocks. This was very different to walking on the metal girders. The one metre square sandstone blocks that comprise the pylons were rough in texture and the outer layer slippery and eroded.

"Mala," he yelled back, "it's hard work but it's not anything a tough gecko like you can't handle." He was trying to encourage her.

Mala began her descent tentatively.

As she navigated the second block a small chunk of sandstone dislodged and she hung by her three remaining claws. Jet caught his breath as Mala caught her feet and proceeded. *Was it a good idea to bring her along?* Jet thought to himself but he knew he needed Mala's help to keep focused.

By the time they were half way down, both geckos were quite adept at the difficult climb and revelled in it's challenges. The approaching ground signalled a different set of emotions. This was human territory and the consequences were still unknown.

The grass grew thick against the pylon wall and Mala's body became instantly hidden in it's foliage. Mala's emerald body was camouflaged but Jet's mottled red colouring was highly visible. Mala and Jet had not touched grass before and were surprised by its gentle texture compared to the sterile grey metal of the bridge.

"So Mr Explorer. Where do we go from here?" queried Mala.

Jet adopted a false sense of confidence.

"The base of the pylon is only about twenty metres long and thirty metres wide, so let's look around it," he suggested.

Jet led Mala along the sandstone wall about twenty centimetres above the grass. They were more vulnerable here but at least they could view their surroundings. Time was of the essence as their absence from the dormitory could soon be discovered.

The adrenaline flowed and their spirits were high. As they rounded the third wall Jet saw a small metal grate ahead.

"What does that say Mala?"

Mala's human language skills were useful.

"Electrical Control Box – Discontinued Use."

Jet smiled "Translated, I think that reads – Jet please enter."

"Be careful!" Mala warned.

"Aren't you coming?"

"Of course I am," Mala said reluctantly.

The tunnel led to the right and then proceeded downwards. It was dimly lit but easily navigated.

Tentatively they crept down the tunnel and were confronted with another bend from which noise echoed. This must be it. Jet held his foot to his mouth indicating quiet. Mala followed closely as Jet peered with one large eye around the bend. In the shadows a large gecko stood in front of a small metal door.

Jet led Mala back out of the tunnel to talk to her.

"What did you see?" Mala gasped.

"There is a large gecko guarding a door. We need to distract him and get the key."

"How do we do that Einstein?" Mala spoke sarcastically because she was scared.

"We need to entice him out here. I know!" Jet told her his plan.

"Who goes there?" The guard jumped as a soft drink can came rolling down the tunnel towards him. The guard dropped the keys and fought hard to keep the can from pinning him to the doorway. He grumbled and began to push the can back towards the entrance.

"Damn human garbage. Why can't humans be cleaner?" he grumbled.

Obviously a similar thing had happened before because the entrance was exposed. Jet was proud of his idea. Jet and Mala had hidden in a side passage and watched the silhouette of the grumbling guard push the can back towards the exit.

After he passed they crept back towards the metal door and the keys which lay on the ground.

"Quickly, I really don't like this," whispered Mala.

"I'm going as fast as I can." Jet fumbled with the keys trying to find the one that fitted the prison door.

"We've only got five minutes!"

*Clink.* The door opened and a two metre long, damp corridor stood before them. There were four small doors on each side of the corridor that must house the prisoners.

Jet muffled his voice and called out, "Geera."

No answer.

"Geera, are you here? It's Sam's son, Jet."

"Jet?" came the surprised reply.

"Yeah. Where are you? We need to talk to you."

"Third door along the corridor on the right."

*Clink!* The door swung open to reveal a small withered gecko in the corner.

"How did you get here?" questioned Geera.

"There's no time for that. When do you get out of here?"

"Not for another four months Jet."

"That's too long."

"For what?" demanded Geera.

"To find my Dad. I need to find him. Do you know where he is?"

"I don't know Jet. I don't know if he made it."

"Made it where?"

"South America. To *Tierra Del Gecko.*" Jet and Mala looked confused. "The ancient Land of the Geckos." Geera elaborated.

"What? Where?"

They could hear the guard returning.

"Go and see Scully. Tell him I sent you," Geera commanded.

"Scully who?"

"Scully the water rat. He lives near the Jeffrey Street Wharf. Ask around, you will find him."

"Thanks Geera."

A large shadow appeared behind Jet and Mala.

"Hey! What are you doing here?" bellowed the guard.

His oversized gecko limbs seized Mala and Jet.

Mala was petrified and Jet was shocked.

"Who are you?" roared the guard.

"I'm Jet. It's all my fault we're here. Leave Mala alone."

"Jet. Is that you?"

"What?" Jet was confused.

"It's Stryker." The guard dropped Jet and Mala and pointed at himself.

"Stryker?"

"Jet, you shouldn't be here," cautioned Stryker the Guard.

Jet and Stryker were friends from gecko school. Jet had saved his life once when a gull had attacked them while they were playing.

"I haven't seen you for ages!"

"You know Stryker?" Geera questioned. "Stryker looks after me in here. If it wasn't for him I would not have survived the last eight months."

Stryker stiffened. "What are you doing Jet? If one of the chief guards comes down here we will all be in trouble."

Jet and Mala explained the whole situation and Geera filled in the blanks they did not know.

Stryker was sympathetic to their cause and he was truly bored with his current position. They decided there and then that they would begin the quest. The quest to find Jet's father and discover *Tierra Del Gecko*. All for one and one for all!

"So where do we start?" queried Jet.

Stryker knew the area around the prison. "Go back to the colony. I will meet you in a week and take you to the water's edge. I know of Scully, the water rat, but I have not met him. My work shift changes next week and I will have time to assist you in your quest."

"Are you sure you want to do this?"

"Yeah. My life is boring; I need a change like this to shake me up. Let's meet on the outer side of this pylon. I don't want you coming back here. The other guard is mean and if he sees you here he will not hesitate to lock you up and throw away the key."

Jet and Mala bid Geera farewell and he in turn wished them well on their quest.

"So we meet one week from today on the outer side of this pylon, two hours after first light," said Stryker.

"Done!" Jet and Mala scurried back as fast as their legs could travel. They hoped nobody had woken and reported them missing.

# 3. The Water Rat

The next week seemed to go slower than the previous whole year. Jet was agitated and anxious. His patience was tested but he had a goal which helped calm him.

Finally the day was upon them. It took their small legs twenty minutes before they reached the tricky sandstone pillars that supported the 52,800 tonnes of steel in the framework of the bridge.

They were slow this morning but still managed to reach the base exactly two hours after sunrise as they had planned. Stryker's large burly frame leant upon the lowest sandstone block as he awaited their arrival. "Thanks for coming Stryker. This means a lot to me."

"That's cool Jet. It has been a real buzz this week. Just thinking about ridding my life of boredom has meant a lot to me too."

"Let's go then," Jet cheered. Stryker led them through the thick grass towards the harbour's edge.

"Hurry up you two. We have to be fast through this section or we will end up as seagull food," Stryker encouraged the others. Mala's heart beat rapidly and her wicked sense of adventure now gave way to a feeling of fear. Jet brought up the rear and his agile limbs had no trouble with the various obstacles.

The trio made it to the safety of a harbour-side garden that bloomed with red Grevillea flowers. Only twenty metres separated them from their goal, the harbour foreshore, but they still had to descend the grassy bank and cross an exposed roadway.

"Wow, the Harbour Bridge is high from this angle!" Jet remarked as he looked skywards.

"The road on the bridge is forty nine metres above the harbour and the arch of the bridge reaches one hundred and thirty metres from the water's surface," added Mala with an intelligence that impressed her companions.

"How do you know all this?" Stryker asked inquisitively.

"I can read the human's language and it says so on the plaque over there."

Jet and Stryker nodded their heads as they realised how much of an asset Mala was to have around.

Suddenly, directly above them, a large Rainbow Lorikeet flew into the Grevillea bush to feed on the nectar. The bird was as large as a seagull but was coloured like a rainbow in shades of red, green and blue. It squawked musically as it rustled the leaves above them. The Geckos were fascinated but also scared by the bird's similarity to the dangerous seagulls. Their pulses raced and they needed to escape. Because of their inexperience, they didn't realise that all birds were not their enemies.

"Let's go," encouraged Jet.

The three geckos leapt from the rock they were on, rounded another bush and ran headlong into a large lizard.

"And where do you think you're going, mate?" questioned a lizard in a drawling Australian accent.

"Who are you?" demanded Jet.

"Well I'm not trouble, but I am curious." He circled them in a slow waddle. "You're geckos aren't you?"

"Yes."

"Well I'm Beno, the blue tongue lizard." Beno's tongue rolled as he spoke and they could see his long blue tongue.

All three nodded, they were stunned into silence by Beno's size and his enormous belly.

"You're a long way from home. We don't get geckos around these parts much. Normally, they are quiet little creatures and very shy," Beno commented.

"Not all of us," Jet stated proudly in order to separate himself from the more conservative colony members.

"A feisty one! That's good to see," laughed Beno.

"We're adventurers." Jet was getting way too confident.

"I met a feisty one like you a while ago. You remind me of him," Beno reminisced.

"Have you met bridge geckos before?" queried Jet.

"Of course I have." Beno fell silent and tried to recall exactly when it was. "Yeah, during that hot summer we had a year ago, a Gecko with a fiery red tail came this way. I think his name was Sultan, or Sega, or something like that."

"Sultan, I don't know any Sultan. Do you Stryker?" Jet was puzzled.

"No. Never met a Sultan."

"Do you mean Sam?" Mala was definitely a more lateral thinker.

"Sam?" Jet looked shocked.

"Yeah Sam, that's him. Good guy, we had some great conversations. Don't know what happened to him after he left here. Stayed a few days then moved on. He talked a lot about South America."

Jet's eyes lowered and all three geckos went silent.

"That was my Dad." Jet was sad but could not contain his curiosity. "Where did he go when he left you?"

"He was heading to the water's edge, said something about a boat," Beno revealed.

"Where's South America?" Stryker inquired.

"Let me think. The way he was talking I think it must have been far away. Probably on the other side of Sydney Harbour somewhere."

"Really?" Jet was intrigued.

Beno was proud of his worldly knowledge even if it was slightly misguided.

"Where have you been all your life? We blue tongue lizards know things like this. South America is probably in the city somewhere. I think it may even be that large building over there, that large one shaped like a flower on a stick," Beno said pointing out Sydney's Centrepoint Tower.

"Thanks," chorused the three geckos.

"Would you like some lunch while you're here?" Beno asked politely.

"Not today Beno, we haven't got time. Thanks anyway. We have to get to the water's edge and then back by dinner. Maybe some other time," Jet promised.

Beno was a friendly creature but the day was getting on.

"Watch out for those cars," Beno yelled as they left.

The anxious geckos made a dash across the five metres of road that divided the garden from the harbourside. As they reached the edge they leapt over the wall for what they thought was safety.

"Arrhhhhhh," Stryker heard the screams ahead of him but it was too late, he was airborne.

Bang! Bang! Bang! Jet hit the ground, Mala tumbled into Jet, and Stryker rolled into them both.

The bundle of geckos landed at the foot of a large hairy rat perched motionless at the harbour's edge. His size was daunting but his face appeared quite passive. He was a water rat with light brown fur, a long rippled tail, a small sailor hat on his head and a tobacco pipe sticking out of his mouth.

The rat laughed aloud at the commotion that had unfolded at his feet. He shook as he stood, then held his hairy belly and released a guttural laugh that caused his stomach to hurt.

He eventually regained composure and drawled, "Arrr me little land lovers, what ye be doing in these here parts?"

"We've come to visit the water's edge," said Mala, shaken and trapped by the weight of Stryker's body lying across her tail.

"Get off Stryker, you big lug," Mala commanded in a high-pitched voice.

"So ye be geckos from the bridge up yonder," said the water rat in his seafaring tone.

"Well yes. I'm Jet, this is Mala and he's Stryker." Jet felt embarrassed because all the creatures they met seemed to know about them and yet the colony and it's inhabitants were so ignorant of the outside world.

"Oi be Scully." He took off his sailor hat and bowed to the three tiny geckos.

Stryker brought his foot over his mouth and whispered to Jet, "Water rats don't eat geckos, do they?"

"No they don't lad," Scully answered the loud whisper, "your skin is too tough and those beady eyes make me queasy. We don't see many geckos in these parts, haven't seen one in years."

"Geera told us to find you. He said you would have information that could lead us to Sam," Jet ventured.

"Yeah, I remember Geera and Sammy Boy, two geckos with hearts for adventure who said they was going to South America."

"Is that across the other side of the harbour?" Stryker asked.

# 4. The Treasure Map

Scully could not contain his laughter at the youthful innocence of the three geckos.

"No lad, South America is a different continent. It takes ten minutes to cross Sydney Harbour on a ferry boat, and twenty eight days in a much larger container ship to cross the Pacific Ocean and reach South America."

"Twenty eight days," repeated Stryker. "Wow, it must be a long way!"

"When I was younger I used to stow away on big container ships and visit all the smelly ports of the world. I spent many a month travelling up and down the seaports of the West Coast of South America. Guaquil in Ecuador, Lima in Peru and Santiago in Chile, just to name a few," Scully reminisced. "Those were the days... running down the long ropes to be first ashore as the ship docked. Fossicking through the markets for decaying food scraps. Ohhhh, those South Americans put a lot of chilli in their food. I can still vividly remember the heartburn...the pain of over-indulgence. I'd have wind for three weeks after docking in any South American port. The confined conditions on the ships meant other rats were far from impressed. I'd stink like you would not believe, and..."

"Yeah Yeah, we get the picture, thanks Scully," Jet stopped him as the other two geckos winced at the thought.

Jet realised that the sky was turning red and that the sun would set in about an hour.

"We have to go Scully, we have to make it back to the bridge or we will be in trouble."

Scully's eyes narrowed. "I gather you came for the map?"

Mala stopped in her suction tracks. "The map that you gave Sam?"

"The copy of the map that Sammy left me in case he didn't return. It's a treasure map leading to the Land of the Geckos in South America. He called it *Tierra Del Gecko*."

Jet was excited. "Tell me more Scully."

"Not now Jet, we have to go, look the sun's almost down." Mala was always level headed enough to keep them out of danger. "We'll return early tomorrow......... but now we must go!"

"I wouldn't be arguing with that woman," Scully winked at Jet.

"Can we meet you here tomorrow Scully?" Jet asked anxiously.

"Sure, here or down under the ferry wharf lads."

"Thanks. Nice to meet you," Stryker said politely as they left.

The tired geckos ran back across the road, along the garden wall, and across the grass. They were concealed this time as the light had faded and the shadows hid their movements. The only one who stood out was Stryker, who trampled the top of the grass, like a bulldozer. They scampered up the sandstone pylon which by now was difficult to see as the sun had already set. Luckily Sydney has many small suns, ones that radiate from the cars, buildings and streetlights, all of which aided the gecko's safe return.

There was a nervous hush on the pylon wall before the three geckos returned. General Vorax had discovered that they were missing. He was not happy. There was a heavy tension in the air as Jet, Stryker and Mala rounded the last metal girder for the safety of the dark sandstone wall they called home.

"Where have you been?" scolded one of the elderly geckos.

Jet was quick to reply, "Just over to the south pylon." Jet was the best liar of the three and the only one who could keep a straight face.

Tokay was there and eyed him suspiciously.

"I'm not sure I believe you Jet."

"Why would I leave the bridge? It's scary out there," Jet lied.

The silence appeared to last forever.

"I will be keeping a very close eye on you three.... No more chances. Next time the full weight of the detention committee will be thrust upon you," warned General Vorax.

Mala gulped, Stryker left for the prison guard housing and Jet stood defiantly.

"Tell others where you're going next time. Your families were worried sick," scolded the old gecko.

Mala, Jet and Stryker whispered quietly to each other before retiring for the night.

Jet went to see his mother, Teka, before going on night watch. She could sense something strange in his persona that night, so she came close to his side.

"What's troubling you Jet?" Teka asked in a smooth caring tone.

"Tell me about my father," Jet replied.

Teka's eyes closed and turned away and Jet sensed his mother's sorrow.

"He was a wonderful gecko.... strong, proud and a born leader. He had the stars in his eyes and adventure in his heart. He strayed from the bridge one day and he never returned."

"Where did he go Mother?"

"Nobody knows."

"You do Mother!" Jet stared into her eyes not allowing Teka to hide her secret any longer. "You know where he went!"

She tried to hide her shock, but then realised that Jet had acquired knowledge that day to arouse new suspicion.

"Where were you today Jet?" his mother asked quietly.

"We went to the water's edge under the north pylon. I met a blue-tongue lizard and a water rat who had both met my father. They talked about South America."

"His wild dreams," Jet's mother sighed. "He had acquired a map of South America which had a large snake wrapped around a golden gecko. He was determined to find the home of the geckos or *Tierra Del Gecko* as he called it, and to take us all to this mystical land."

"He never returned from South America did he?"

"No Jet, he never returned. I worry that you are like your father. That's why I did not tell you sooner. I was afraid I would lose you too." Tears formed in his mother's large eyes.

Jet did not tell Teka that Scully had a copy of the map. If it turned out favourably, he would tell her later.

The sun was just about to rise the next day when Mala, Stryker and Jet met again and busily scampered off. A quick breakfast of insects caught in the many cavities of the bridge and a quiet discussion about the map could not contain their anticipation of what lay ahead. By six thirty in the morning they had already began retracing their route to Scully's harbour-side home. Back down the north pylon, across the grass, along the flowerbed, across the road and onto the slimy harbour side wall.

"Nobody is here."

Jet was scouring the wall with his eyes and even looked into the nearest storm water pipe.

"He's probably at the wharf," Mala recalled.

They ran along the rock wall, occasionally scaring a small crab or two, and then bounded onto the wooden under-story of the wharf.

"Jeffrey Street Ferry Wharf." Mala studied the sign.

"There's Scully." Stryker pointed sideways with his front foot. His balance was so upset by the excitement he slipped off the wooden beam and into the water. *Plunk!* A splash of water rose up and covered Jet and Mala. They could not see their friend as the water surface teemed with bubbles. Stryker had never been in water before and had no idea how to swim. As the bubbles cleared they could see Stryker's distressed face staring skyward from below the surface. His thick gecko arms waved about frantically and small bubbles escaped from his wide mouth.

Jet and Mala could not swim either and felt helpless as more and more bubbles escaped from Stryker's mouth.

"Help, Scully, help," Mala yelled.

Scully raced over and sized up the situation immediately. He leapt from the beam and dived nose first into the salty Harbour water. The seconds felt like hours as Mala and Jet peered into the green murky depths, frightened for their friend's safety.

The water exploded as Scully surfaced and gasped for air. Stryker's limp body was held delicately in Scully's mouth. He quickly swam towards the rocky edge as Jet and Mala followed higher up on the beams. Scully placed Stryker's body face up delicately and began to breathe air into his mouth. No reaction was seen at first as Stryker's body lay motionless. Then suddenly a gurgling sound erupted from within Stryker's stomach and a fountain of water was released from his mouth.

"He's alive," shrieked Mala!

Jet let out a sigh of relief and wiped the sweat from his brow.

"You scared us Stryker." Jet turned to Scully with a smile of appreciation, "Thanks for rescuing him Scully."

Stryker sat up but remained weak for the next half hour as Scully entertained them with some of the dangerous adventures he had narrowly escaped from over the years.

"Let's go back to my place, you land lovers need somewhere dry." Scully led the way back to a storm water pipe on the harbourside wall. It was a metre wide concrete pipe that had a dribble of water flowing from it's dark interior. It took the geckos some time to adjust to the dark conditions and the pungent aromas. They desperately tried to keep up with Scully's rapid pace as he raced along the familiar surface. He turned right about ten metres along the larger pipe and into a dry, smaller pipe that was about one quarter the size of the original. The smaller pipe came to an abrupt end at a collapsed rubble heap.

"Well it's not much, but it's home," Scully said proudly.

There was a straw bed in the middle and the walls had been excavated to accommodate the possessions Scully had accumulated during his life of adventure. There was a small urn from the Middle East, a one-cent coin picturing George Washington from New York, a shark tooth from the Philippines, a spice jar from Zanzibar and a flute from the South American Indian tribes.

Jet surveyed the scene quickly and was disappointed.

"Would you like a cup of tea?" Scully offered.

"No thanks," Jet shrugged.

"Jet what's up?"

"Aw nothing. I just think we are wasting our time. There's no map here."

"Ahhh me friend of little patience," Scully winked. He turned his back on the geckos and levered a special stone on the back wall that uncovered a hidden cavity.

"You don't think I would leave me prized possessions out here for all to take?"

Jet was embarrassed. Scully had just saved his friend's life and he already distrusted him.

Scully struck a match and ignited a small lantern. They followed him into the hole and what appeared to be a cavern similar to Aladdin's fabled treasure cave. The trinkets in the previous room were worthless compared to Scully's hidden collection. This was magnificent.

The light from the lantern radiated off the gold, silver and jewels. The astonished geckos spent the next ten minutes wandering around in silence as they absorbed the pure majesty of this secret stash. There was a gold sovereign from a Spanish Galleon, a jewelled Aztec necklace and a diamond ring bigger than Mala's eye. In the corner was a bracelet encrusted with emeralds and sapphires with the insignia of an Indian royal family and all around were coins from every corner of the globe. An intricately woven Persian rug kept the precious collection from ever touching the ground. Jet was impressed, but it was the map in the corner tied with gold ribbon that attracted his attention the most.

"What do you think?" Scully's pride in his collection was evident in his voice.

"It's beautiful Scully," Mala stated in wonder.

"Wow!" was all that Stryker could repeatedly mutter.

"You are a man of many hidden talents Scully," complimented Jet. "Now can I see the map please?"

Mala and Stryker covered themselves in expensive jewellery from around the room and laughed as they paraded like royalty.

Jet and Scully settled into one corner and unravelled the old scroll. Scully had not looked at the map in quite a while and the paper was fragile and browning with decay. The map showed very little detail, but the town names and colourful drawing still indicated direction and geographical locations. The map did not mention South America but used La Paz as it's main reference point. Scully informed Jet that La Paz was the capital of a land-locked country named Bolivia. By this stage Mala and Stryker had circled around, fascinated by the story that was unfolding.

The map would lead the faithful explorers from La Paz, to a mountainous area drawn around the city's name, and on to an abrupt end in the Northern Amazonian Jungle. The "X", meaning the final point of discovery, was a craggy, cloudy peak along the river, *Rio Beni.*

Scully translated the Spanish parts of the map. He pointed out the town of Rurrenabaque and the Beni River, a tributary of the mighty Amazon River. Nearby was a craggy peak, below the peak was a cave and inside the cave lived a large serpent wrapped around a Golden Gecko. The map was called "*Tierra Del Gecko*" which translated to "The land of the Geckos". Jet now realised why his father had left.

# 5. The Commitment

"I'm going to find this place," Jet stated with resolve and looked for the backing of his two closest friends. "You should come too Scully, you'll be a great asset."

Mala and Stryker's eyes met but they remained silent. It was a large adventure just to come down off the bridge, let alone go to an unknown country called Bolivia.

"Jet… I'm not capable of those types of adventures any more. I have a sore right leg from an old injury and I like the comforts of home now. I have my memories, but I appreciate the offer. Besides this place is '*Tierra Del Gecko*', not '*Tierra Del Water Rat*'," Scully smiled.

Stryker's face hardened with resolve. "If you go Jet, I'm coming too." Stryker was an old friend and liked the sound of adventure almost as much as Jet. "I need your protection as much as you need mine."

Mala was undecided. She had two sisters and a close family bond. Her mind raced wildly. Jet and Stryker did not interrupt but allowed her time to reflect. She raised her eyes and looked directly at her friends. With a large grin and wicked curiosity in her eyes she announced, "Life around here would be too boring without the two of you. Besides, I'm the one who gets both of you out of trouble, so I have to come along." Mala brimmed with excitement.

"How will we do this?" Jet asked Scully.

"First, you will have to find a ship going to South America, preferably Peru." Scully's mind was very logical. "You will need maps to get over the Andean Mountains from Peru to Bolivia, then your treasure map will lead the way from there."

"Scully, what's the difference between one of these ferries and a ship?" Stryker asked.

Scully chuckled. "A container ship is what you'll have to catch lads, they are about one hundred and twenty metres long and weigh over fifty thousand tonnes. You must have seen those large ships that appear to only just squeeze under the Harbour Bridge?"

"They leave from many ports. The largest port is Botany Bay. I have a friend who's a Pelican, he'll find out for us. The ships have their homeport written on the stern. Pelican Pete has connections everywhere. If there is a ship going to Peru, Pete will know or be able to find out. Trust me!"

Mala was getting excited.

"He lives above the wharf just here. Would you like to see him now?"

"I'm keen," Jet look at Scully for approval.

"Then there's no better time. Let's go visit me old mate Pelican Pete!" Scully rose off the ground, sealed up the secret entrance and they all proceeded out of the pipe. It was midday now and the sunshine was bright in their eyes.

When they found him, Pelican Pete was asleep on top of a large white wooden post at the end of the ferry wharf. Scully led them back along the harbour-side wall to the wooden beams under the Jeffrey Street Wharf.

Stryker was still shaken from his near drowning ordeal. "If it's all the same with you guys, I'll stay here."

"Okay, we won't be long," Jet reassured him.

Scully, Mala and Jet proceeded out along the beams until they got close to the end.

Pelican Pete was an enormous white bird, with a long beak and droopy looking chin. His chin was like a scoop net which helped him catch fish. Pelican Pete had a distinct black ring around one eye and some called him 'Black Eyed Pete'.

"Yo Pete."

"Who said that?" Pelican Pete questioned in a deep, slow voice as his beady eyes scoured the landscape. He jumped to his feet and circled slowly.

"Pete, down here," Scully waved his front paw and Pelican Pete peered over.

"Hello my little furry friend. How are you Scully?" His tone was almost musical. "And who are your little friends?"

"I'm Jet and this is Mala," Jet said.

"Remember that gecko we helped a year ago, the little land lover with the red tail? He was going to South America on a container boat."

Pete thought hard, and you could see his eyes register when he finally remembered Jet's Dad. "Yeah, fiery red tail and doing it all alone."

"Well, we need your help again. These two and their friend are also looking for a container boat bound for Peru. Can you find out when the next one leaves Pete?"

Pelican Pete enjoyed helping others and was glad to do a good turn.

"You'll have to give me three days, there are a few ports to check and my cousins will no doubt want me to stay over in Botany Bay. I'll plan to be back here on Thursday. How's that?"

"Thanks Pete," Mala said in a soft voice and Pete blushed.

"We'll all meet back here Thursday," Scully said as he thanked Pete.

Scully tuned out then sniffed the air. The pungent odour of rotten fish wafted their way.

"Sorry. Have to leave now. Come to my place on Thursday and we will go see Pete." Scully scampered off in the direction of the smell.

"Thanks," Mala and Jet chorused.

Pelican Pete stretched out his metre and a half wingspan and flew off across the Harbour with more grace than Jet or Mala would have given him credit for.

"Wow! Look at Pete," yelled Jet.

He had spoken too soon because Pete flew headfirst into the side of the ferry.

Mala gasped. Jet lent forward but could do little to help.

"Are you alright?" Jet yelled.

Pete floated on his stomach and nursed his injured head.

It was amusing to see Pete's entire wingspan spread over his head as he rubbed it slowly.

"I think Pete and Stryker will get on very well," laughed Mala.

Jet and Mala joined Stryker as he soaked up the afternoon sun and watched the shimmering reflection off the water's surface. They told him the plan and half an hour later began to retrace their steps to the North Pylon of the Harbour Bridge.

The eager geckos found it hard to settle over the next few days. They wanted to tell the entire gecko colony about their planned adventure to '*Tierra Del Gecko*', but realised that they could not. Three days felt like an entire year. On that Thursday morning Jet, Stryker and Mala had all congregated at the outskirts of the colony. Vorax's guards had followed them over the previous few days, but they had managed to elude them today. Their fitness had improved dramatically from the epic voyages to and from the water's edge, and later they would realise the true advantage of this.

Off they went again, down the pylon, across the grass, along the garden bed, across the road and up the storm water pipe.

The pipe was pitch black and they stood outside it's entrance and peered in. Nobody wanted to lead, as the pipe looked larger and more fearsome without Scully leading the way. Jet pushed Stryker to the front, then Stryker pushed Mala and finally Mala pushed Jet back to the lead.

"Go on then!" Stryker challenged Jet, as he laughed nervously.

Jet led the way into the dark, smelly pipe. He had only travelled three metres into the pipe, but the southern facing angle of the entrance caused the area to be almost devoid of sunlight.

"Scully?" Jet yelled apprehensively. They did not know what else lived in the pipe. "Scully! Scully! Are you there?"

Up in the distance Jet saw a glowing red light approach. He could not work out if the glow came from two beady eyes or a single piercing flame. Scully definitely did not have red eyes. The feature got closer and the glow increased with intensity and flared brightly every few seconds. Mala and Stryker stepped up to Jet's side and witnessed the object as it approached. The footsteps from the beast resonated loudly down the pipe as the creature stamped heavily into the watery ground. The glow rose again and a 'whooshing' sound followed. The three geckos could not retreat fast enough; they stumbled over each other as they retreated to the entrance of the pipe.

"Where are you going me little landlubbers?"

It was Scully's voice. As he advanced they could see his tobacco pipe was alight and he had come to greet them.

"You scared us Scully. This storm pipe makes you sound like a giant monster," Mala laughed and released her nervous tension.

"Arr, you'll come across many a meaner monster than me in South America, mark my words."

Scully's comment was brief but you could tell there was a definite warning in his words.

"Let's go see Clumsy Pete…I mean Pelican Pete." Scully directed them all out of the pipe.

Pelican Pete sat in his usual spot and looked quite tired. Scully got his attention again and they settled down to a conversation.

"Did you find a ship Pete?" Mala brought the conversation back on track.

"Sure did," Pete announced with pride. "The S.S.Huaraz leaves for Lima tomorrow at 0900."

Planning the adventure excited the enterprising geckos but the fact that they now had an imminent departure created a new daunting prospect.

"That's nine in the morning tomorrow isn't it?" Stryker replied with a frightened sense of urgency.

"That's right Stryker," Mala confirmed, deep in thought.

"I did some more research. If you catch bus number four five three across the bridge it will get you to Wynyard Station. You will have to change there to bus number one three seven that will drop you within a kilometre of container terminal number twelve. There you have to board the S. S. Hauraz at least half an hour before it leaves port. That's eight thirty am."

Pelican Pete may be clumsy but he sure was smart. They thanked him for the advice and all three retreated back to Scully's pipe to plan their next twenty four hours.

"It's too soon," Mala opened the conversation.

"It's now or never," Jet blurted out.

"Calm down my friends. Come, sit over here, I need to tell you some things," Scully said smoothly.

Scully was concerned about the gullibility and innocence of the three geckos. Over the next two hours he described at great length the dangers that they would encounter and warned them of the risks of travel. Scully's knowledge was deep and his words were wise. The trio of geckos sat transfixed by every word that Scully muttered and only occasionally interrupted to acquire more insight. In the end all three were convinced. They would leave tomorrow.

# 6. The Dagger of Danger

Scully retreated into his treasure cavity and retrieved the map and a small dagger. The dagger, five centimetres in length, was encased in a solid leather sheath. Once exposed, they could see it's finely crafted blade and the jewel encrusted handle. The centre jewel was of unknown origin, surrounded by many smaller rubies and sapphires.

"This is the *Dagger of Danger*. I was given this by a wise old rat in the port of Shanghai, China. I saved his life, and in return he gave me this". The geckos stared in wonder. "When danger is near, the jewel will light up red, and when all is calm the jewel will stay green." With great symbolism Scully handed it to Jet. "I should have given this to your father. Take it and walk wisely." Jet was astonished by Scully's kind gift and thoughtful words.

Jet strapped the dagger and sheath to his back and tucked the map underneath. Then they bid Scully farewell and left to spend their final night on the bridge. On the journey back no one spoke, each of the geckos needed time to seek out their personal thoughts. How were they going to break the news to their families and the colony? Nearing the top of the north pylon Jet halted and turned to face Mala and Stryker.

"I have been thinking about what we can tell the others, we can either slip away quietly in the early morning or call a meeting tonight and tell them all." Jet was undecided. "Let's vote."

"All those in favour of sneaking away quietly…"

No foot was raised.

"All those in favour of calling a meeting…"

All three were unanimous.

"I want to tell my family first," Stryker said.

"I think that is a good idea," Jet reassured him.

They strode around the last corner of the sandstone pylon with determination on their faces. Everyone in the gecko colony noticed their return and in particular the dagger and roll of paper strapped to Jet's back. The guards moved forward in a gesture of aggression. The three geckos's stood their ground. Tension built in the air. Were Jet, Stryker and Mala going to be imprisoned? All eyes turned to General Vorax who was stony faced and silent.

"Wait" General Vorax commanded "Let them talk".

The stern faces of Jet, Mala and Stryker were confident and a hush fell over the entire colony. Jet broke the silence and announced there would be a colony meeting at sunset and all were to attend.

"So be it" General Vorax conceded. He had seen this determination and arrogance previously in Jet's father, Sam.

Jet greeted his Mother, Teka, with the usual touching of noses, then moved away and stared straight into her eyes.

"You're going after your father, aren't you Jet?" His mother was very perceptive.

"Yes, Mother."

"You are so like him." Teka paused. "I only hope you find what you are looking for."

Jet's mother had to stop talking as she broke down in tears.

Jet's eyes lowered and he stared at the hard metal surface. "I will return Mother, I promise."

Teka did not reply. Those were almost the exact words uttered by his father Sam when he had left her. His Mother knew something like this would happen one day, but had dreaded the time when it would come.

The gecko's meeting started as the last beams of sunlight reflected down the length of the Parramatta River. Jet, Stryker and Mala stood defiantly in front of the group. Jet took a step forward.

"I would like to inform you all that Mala, Stryker and I are going off in search of the great *Land of the Gecko,*" Jet held the map aloft and told everyone they were going to Bolivia, a country in South America. All the geckos fell silent.

"I did not know where South America was until recently, but it's a twenty eight day journey in a great ship across the Pacific Ocean," Jet continued. Some geckos were shocked, partly at the distance, but mostly due to their ignorance of what he was talking about. Some had already dismissed the absurd adventure as ludicrous and moved away from the meeting. The elders stayed and wanted to see the map. General Vorax wanted to see the map. Jet conceded and let them view the ancient scroll. Lengthy discussions followed and eventually the blessings were given even from the elders who considered the journey a suicide mission. As a leader General Vorax hoped they would find this ancient land and possibly a better life for the colony. However for now he was glad to see Jet go from the colony as Jet stirred up too many rebellious feelings amongst the group. Jet would go and the colony would return to it's strict regime.

It was with a mixture of excitement and apprehension that Jet, Stryker and Mala agreed to spend the night with their families and meet at sunrise. Sleep was sporadic and the air was electric. The adrenaline was pumping through their bodies well before sunrise, when the three met again. They bid their families goodbye and were touched that most of the colony had amassed to wish them a safe journey.

Jet, Mala and Stryker strode across the metal beams of the roadway until they had reached the one directly over the express bus lane. Here they sat at a vantage point where they could watch the bus numbers from a distance of one hundred metres. Beams blocked some of their view and they were keenly aware that the buses would be frantic. A bus travelling at approximately sixty kilometres per hour would only take about six seconds from the time they saw it to when it was directly beneath them. They stood side by side along the beam so that they could all leap within the one second 'window of opportunity' they had.

"You'll jump first Stryker, then Mala and finally me," Jet had decided. "The bus is about fifteen metres long so we'll have enough room for all of us to land on it's flat roof."

They attempted to guess the distance when the first bus passed under. It had to be at least three metres and then they had to allow for the wind factor and falling velocity, of which none of the three geckos had any idea.

"Just jump when I say, OK?" Jet was trying to remain calm. "This is our only opportunity and if we miss it, we could miss the container ship."

Bus after bus went under the staring geckos but it was the tenth bus that finally caught Mala's eye.

"It's a four five three, a four five three," Mala yelled excitedly. The seconds ticked away as the bus approached.

"Ready Stryker?" Jet questioned.

Stryker gave the foot up to show he was ready.

"Go Stryker!" Jet yelled.

"Go Mala!"

*Ahhhhhhh.* All three were airborne and headed towards the bus.

Stryker had leapt an instant too early and the roof was not underneath his landing.

*Sppplatttt.*

Stryker's suction-cup feet adhered to the front windscreen of the speeding bus. His face contorted as the G-forces pushed him against the glass pane directly in front of the driver. The driver winced at the site of a flattened gecko trying groggily to recover from the harrowing ordeal. Stryker shook his head, winked at the bus driver and then meandered up the windscreen to the top of the roof. The bus swerved as the driver came to terms with the fact that a gecko had just winked at him.

Mala had landed near the air hatch, which broke her backward movement and allowed for a fairly clean landing. However, Jet had left the Harbour Bridge beam a fraction too late and had rolled down the bus a few times before clinging to the final ten centimetres of roof surface. He scurried up to Mala who was now concerned about Stryker's whereabouts.

"Stryker," she yelled.

Then a figure appeared over the front of the bus, a rather dazed looking Stryker with a blackening eye and a stagger in his walk.

"I'm so glad you're safe Stryker," Mala relaxed.

"If this is just the start Jet, we're in big trouble," Stryker tried to laugh it off.

"Maybe, just maybe," replied Jet.

The three geckos then faced into the wind and took a last look at the Harbour Bridge, Opera House and home.

"Goodbye Sydney Harbour," they all chorused.

The bus weaved in and out of the Sydney streets and came to rest at Wynyard. They quickly spotted the bus numbered one three seven and they scurried across the roofs of four buses to finally alight on the bus they needed. The buses that were temporarily parked at Wynyard station radiated to many of the suburbs that house Sydney's four million plus population.

They had to be at the ship by eight thirty am and once on board bus number one three seven they were annoyed it had not left immediately. It was another ten minutes before the engine roared and the bus departed to their unseen destination. Mala looked up to one of the large buildings and could read the clock. Their bus left at seven am, they had less than two hours before the container ship departed. This bus appeared to take forever to get anywhere in the mounting city traffic. It meandered in and out of every city street imaginable before it snaked it's way further down the coastal suburbs of Eastern Sydney.

"What time do you think it is Mala?" Jet was anxious.

"I don't know. I have not seen a clock tower since we left the city."

Jet decided to walk down the outside window to try and peer at someone's watch on the bus. He licked his sticky feet to get extra traction and walked directly down the side windows of the bus. The first person he saw was wearing a large fluffy jacket that looked like a poodle. She stared back at Jet when he looked in. He poked out his tongue at her and she withdrew in shock. The second was a young child whose watch was concealed by a protective covering. The child opened the window and tried to grab Jet but he scurried away just in time. The third was an old lady with a large wristwatch with easy-to-read numbers.

# 7. The Container Ship Journey

"It's ten past eight, we had better be close or we'll miss the ship," Jet told the others.

Just then the bus rounded a corner and they could see the large ships Pelican Pete had described. The bus pulled to a stop at a small shelter and they jumped off onto the shelter roof. It was an easy feat considering what they had already been through that day. Jet was now careful of the map and dagger as the tumble on the first bus had already bruised his back and he had been close to losing the map. After they ran down the roof they realised they still had a kilometre to the ship, but which was the right one? They had been told to go to terminal number twelve, but each terminal was about five hundred metres apart. Their time was quickly running out. A ship's foghorn blasted from the nearest pier, and they all concluded that this must be the one. They ran and ran, across the gravel road and through the many potholes. They finally reached the large metal gate but it was terminal fourteen and the ship was bound for Hong Kong.

Jet was about to give up hope when Pelican Pete swooped overhead. "Over this way fellows, and hurry," Pete called out.

They ran frantically. They had not eaten breakfast and felt fatigued from limited sleep. They slipped under the large, barbwire gateway and saw that one of the four ropes securing the ship to shore was already removed. They were breathless but still charged onwards towards the nearest rope with a renewed sense of urgency. Their small legs were burning due to the lack of oxygen feeding their limbs and their lungs were wheezing heavily. They were only two metres away from the thick hessian rope and possible safety of the ship. Suddenly the rope sagged lifelessly as the large metal lug that fastened it to the concrete pier was no longer needed and the rope slammed against the ship's side.

"Hurry, there are still two more ropes!" Stryker was now at the front pacing the others with his large muscular legs and considerable stamina.

Above them they saw one of the ship's crew untying the third rope. Stryker quickly bypassed it and headed straight towards the last rope and their final hope of entering the ship. Stryker knew Jet was desperate to catch this ship and unleashed in himself reserves of energy he thought he did not possess. Two tugboats were taking up the tension on the towlines in order to haul the ship away from it's berth.

"Quick, this way!" Stryker yelled.

White water swirled from the giant propeller located at the stern. This was the last rope attached but as they looked upward one of the ship's crew began to untie it's bulk. This would disconnect the rear of the ship from shore and dash the geckos' dreams. Stryker, Jet and Mala covered the last thirty metres of the concrete wharf in record time, leapt onto the metal lug that anchored the rope to shore and began running up the coarse hessian. The tension on the rope became slack under foot and it began to sag.

Finally the rope was disconnected from the shore lug and went crashing towards the ship's side. Stryker, Jet and Mala had only made it two thirds of the way up it's twenty metre length and realised they were on a collision course that swung into the ship's large metal side.

"Just before it hits, jump towards that anchor hole, and hold on," Stryker yelled above the sound of the turbine engines beneath the ship's metal exterior.

*Whoosh, whoosh, splat.*

The geckos plummeted through the circular metal hole that drops the stern anchor chain. Stryker and Mala landed in a bundle on the floor, contorted in amongst the three tonnes of anchor chain.

"Where's Jet?" Stryker asked.

"Help, Help!" Jet yelled.

Jet hung on by one suction pad to a small thread of hessian that dangled in the breeze.

"Hang on, mate," Stryker reassured.

Stryker reached over with his solid grip, linked paws with Jet and held tight. He grunted as he dragged Jet back onto the deck of the ship, then collapsed red-faced in the corner.

"Thanks Stryker." Jet sat up but was unsteady. He brushed himself off and tried to muster enthusiasm.

"Well that was interesting." He looked around. "This must be our new home."

"What a terrible day, it's not even Monday nine o'clock yet," said Mala as she rubbed her head.

"I need some food," were Stryker's next words and his stomach growled in agreement.

Pelican Pete was perched above them and was astonished at their good fortune.

"I followed you all the way from the Harbour Bridge, watching from the air of course. You three really love your adventures. I'm surprised you all made it." Pete was impressed. "The humans drive the ship but water rats run the animal world, make friends fast and mention Scully's name. Scully is still a legend and his name will gain you safe passage. Well, goodbye and good luck."

"Thanks again Pete."

They all waved as Pete spread his wings across Botany Bay and headed back to the Jeffrey Street Wharf and the safety of Sydney Harbour.

"This ship is huge, let's go find a crevasse, eat some bugs, then go explore," Mala suggested.

After a scrumptious breakfast of mosquitoes and flies they sat in the sun to warm their bodies.

"So this is our new home!"

Mala peered around at the new scenery and began to study a metal plaque on the wall behind her.

"What does it say Mala," Jet asked. He and Stryker could not read the human language.

"It's statistical information about the S.S.Huaraz. Apparently this ship is one hundred and twenty metres long, weighs approximately eighty thousand tonnes and can legally hold five to six hundred containers in its cavernous hold. It must have a crew of at least eighteen people and takes up to half a kilometre to come to a halt when at maximum cruising speed. Sounds like a moving version of the Sydney Harbour Bridge."

Apart from the plaque Jet and Stryker could see that the S.S.Huaraz had a few rusty patches but in general the green and white painted ship was in good condition.

The three geckos hugged the walls as they scampered along, always cautious to avoid the humans. They decided to remain at the stern, or back of the ship, as it had the best vantage point. They ran up the walls of the bridge or driver's room, and onto it's roof. Above this were large antenna rods that would allow them panoramic views and their final glimpse of Sydney. The ship began to gain momentum as it powered between the red and green lights of Botany Bay's headlands and out into the vast Pacific Ocean. It was now ten am and Sydney did not have a cloud in the sky. It was a beautiful spring day with the breeze calmly blowing from the southwest at ten kilometres per hour.

"Goodbye Sydney. See you soon." Mala was sentimental as she waved her front foot at the entire city.

"We'll be back in a couple of months," Jet said confidently.

The curvature of the earth eventually obscured Sydney from view about thirty kilometres into their voyage, and it was then that they decided to go and meet the water rats. If Scully was a good indicator, water rats appeared very friendly. But little did the adventurers realise what was in store.

The three geckos descended from the stern antenna, back across the roof of the bridge and down along the deck.

"My guess is they live way down in the deep, dark base of the ship," suggested Stryker, "that is if Scully's little storm drain hide-out is any gauge."

They found the nearest ladder and criss-crossed the metal rungs to maintain a clear view as they began their descent. Two levels down they saw something move in the distance but the light was dim and they could not make out the shape. It appeared to be a large water rat but it scurried off fast.

"Hey wait!" Jet yelled at the diminishing shadow.

Mala, Jet and Stryker headed in the direction from which the shadow had disappeared and found a very long metal corridor. It was over one and a half metres in height and disappeared rapidly into the darkness.

"This area must run along the side of all the containers," Mala guessed. "It will probably go the whole length of the ship."

The walls were painted dull grey and everything was large and metal. They continued into the darkness and were confident that Scully's name would keep them safe once they encountered the leader of the water rats. Occasionally a steam vent hissed, releasing its warm cloudy vapour that further diminished the gecko's vision.

They had covered fifty metres of the eerie, metal corridor, and they could hear the shrieking and rustling sounds ahead. With every step they took the sound grew in volume to a frightening crescendo and the fear on the faces of the geckos intensified. Eventually they rounded a large metal doorway, one with a watertight seal and large circular handle. The three geckos slowly peered around the corner and were shocked by what they saw.

# 8. The Encounter with Sir Typhoid

A wild party was in progress and there were water rats everywhere. An atrocious band played an assortment of instruments that appeared to have been scavenged from a kitchen. Unfortunately the ruckus was amplified through a child's musical toy trumpet to increase the already ear piercing noise.

Rats were everywhere. Some held thimbles of juice and sang with the band while others stood around makeshift tables and argued heatedly. A few very active rats danced to the music in a fashion that looked like they were caught in a tornado. One table had caught Jet's eye. It was constructed from a flat sardine tin and the rats leaning against it had an air of dominance about them. Jet was distracted but was jolted to reality when the music suddenly stopped. The lead singer stared directly at the geckos and this silence caused the rest of the water rats to look in the same direction.

A large, hairy water rat rose from the main table. His fur was a deep glossy brown, one eye was covered with a black patch and there were several tattoos engraved on his muscular forearms and hind legs.

"I knew you were aboard, me little slimy friends." The large rat ground his teeth as he spoke in his distinct sea-faring tone.

"We was waiting for youse to join us and make yourselves known. One of me men spotted youse when youse were talking to that oversized sea gull." The rat was referring to Pelican Pete in a very nasty tone.

Jet, Mala and Stryker slowly revealed their whole bodies from behind the metal door hinges and stood silently.

"Well don't just stand there, come over here and let me have a look at youse".

They did what the large rat had commanded but kept their backs to the wall as they moved in his direction.

"So who gave you the right of passage on my ship, you little reptiles?" The large rat inquired forcefully. His aggressive tone intensified. "And you'll refer to me as Sir Typhoid because once youse have met me, youse will never forget me." He laughed cynically.

The other rats laughed in unison. They had seen these instances before and were anticipating the regular result.

"Well Sir Typhoid," Jet was humble, "A water rat friend of ours named Scully gave us safe passage," Jet kept his head half bowed.

"Scully, Scully, I've never heard of no Scully." Sir Typhoid was agitated, his wide mouth opened to reveal long yellowish fangs that now pointed at the frightened geckos.

He began to circle Jet, who had stepped forward to talk with him.

"Where does this 'Scully' get the right to grant safe passage on my ship?" His voice was building to a nasty climax and saliva started to foam in the corners of his mouth. His muscular forearms rippled and the blood vessels bulged through the fur.

Jet was about to speak when Sir Typhoid silenced him with a wave of his paw and studied the dagger on Jet's back.

"So youse carry a weapon my cold-blooded friend?" queried Sir Typhoid staring at the brightly lit jewelled handle. "Is that for enemies like me?" Sir Typhoid was sarcastic but wondered if the little gecko was practised in the use of the dagger.

The circling continued and Sir Typhoid was getting closer with each circuit. The other rats were attentive, eager for blood. They had seen Sir Typhoid tear apart other freeloaders with a single bite. The saliva dripped from the corner of Sir Typhoid's mouth and his eyes glazed over with an unconscious look of evil.

Mala and Stryker could hardly watch. Their friend was in grave danger. Sir Typhoid had closed in tightly and appeared to be ready for attack when an elderly rat appeared from behind Sir Typhoid. The wise rat whispered in Sir Typhoid's pointed dark ear and Sir Typhoid was attentive. Who was this old grey rat that commanded so much attention? He had a wise persona, intelligent eyes and a hobbled gait aided by a walking cane. The time seemed endless but finally Sir Typhoid's facial expression loosened as he peered back at the anxious geckos. The old rat left Sir Typhoid's side and he raised his paw to get everyone's attention.

"My father has spoken and he tells me this Scully character was an intrepid adventurer and fine friend of his. Your lives will be spared but you had better not cross me." He had to justify his leniency to the other rats. Once you go soft in your actions your command is threatened and Sir Typhoid wanted to stay at the top.

"Nobody is to harm the geckos or they have to deal with me," he threatened. "Now play some Latin music, after all, we're bound for South America."

Sir Typhoid walked away from the Geckos without a backward glance and began a card game at the largest of the tables.

The old grey rat hobbled towards the thankful geckos and introduced himself as Tombar. He appeared older than Scully and explained later that he had been Scully's mentor. Tombar's wisdom was broad like Scully's, and he told the attentive geckos many wonderful stories.

Tombar recommended that they keep out of the water rat's territory and bunk down at the stern of the ship. They heeded this advice and found a dark grey wall under the crews' quarters. The wall was slightly damp, due to the condensation from a steam vent nearby but they were fully protected from the ocean's elements of rain, wind and wave splash. Over the next twenty eight days they rarely encountered the large group of water rats and that suited them immensely. Tombar would come to visit daily, and entertained the geckos with wild sea stories. He also provided them with more current information on the port at Lima in which they would eventually dock.

Stryker and Jet adapted to the gentle swaying of the ship caused by the Pacific Ocean's great power. Mala was not so enthusiastic and quite often had an upset stomach and was not able to keep her food down.

The ocean swell varied only slightly in the first two weeks and never rose over two metres in height. The geckos would sit on the high decks and relax as the wind blew lightly over the bow. These conditions had no effect on the eighty thousand tonne vessel as it ploughed through the waves like a sharp carving knife. It was on day eighteen that this all changed. The light and fluffy cumulus clouds began to darken and rise.

A southerly storm was brewing bringing cold winds and huge waves from the frigid Antarctic Ocean. Within hours the weather had changed to pelting rain, the swell had risen to a daunting seven metres and the wind howled across the deck with a destructive force.

Mala became very seasick and took on the appearance of an Albino gecko.

"Just put me out of my misery," Mala groaned.

"You're not going to die, once the swell drops you'll be fine," Jet reassured her but he had never encountered such horrific conditions before. If the weather was this bad back on the Harbour Bridge pylon all the Geckos would retreat to the safety of the wall but it had never been this bad. Jet was worried but tried to disguise his concerns.

"Come on Stryker, let's go up on deck and see if there's any sign of a break in the weather." Jet was content to let Mala sleep.

The cautious geckos had to ascend the stairs behind the captain's bridge as the normal hatch was closed due to sea spray. They crept up the back window of the bridge and looked through as the ocean unleashed it fury onto the bow of the ship. Their location was protected from the buffeting winds and rain, but they saw clearly what the ocean had to offer. There was no mercy as the pounding waves broke over the bow and exploded across the deck in a flooding torrent. The water had not drained from the deck before the next mighty wave would completely engulf the ship. The power of the ocean was a force that Stryker and Jet now held in deep respect. There was no obvious break in the storm so they retreated back to aid Mala and wait it out. Only once during the four day storm did Tombar come to visit. He was quite frail and it was a long walk in his condition. Content that the three geckos were safe, Tombar went back to his water rat domain. Occasionally Jet and Stryker would venture down into the engine room and lie on the warm metal casing that surrounded the turbines. This would warm them up enough to find food for themselves and the ailing Mala, if she could keep it in her stomach.

It was not until day twenty two that the storm finally subsided and the seas took on a glassy calm. Mala felt much better and was always cautious to avoid the sordid lair of the water rats. They all decided to venture across the top deck to the front of the ship. After a hearty breakfast of grubs, the jubilant geckos strolled along the walls of the ship and soaked up the sun's warmth.

Mala's spirit was revitalised and she shrieked with joy as a pod of bottle-nose dolphins rode the ship's bow waves.

"This is beautiful Jet. I would never have come if you had not been so pushy," Mala smiled.

"What do you think of the adventure so far Stryker?" asked Jet.

"Well, I did some deep thinking during that storm. If all the adrenaline packed episodes I have encountered so far in my life had to flash before my eyes, I think this adventure would take up most of it. However, I might add, I have never been in so many life threatening situations until I met you," he said pointing at Jet and laughing.

The end of the voyage was fast approaching and the corresponding number of visits Tombar made to the geckos increased. He was concerned about his new lizard friends and felt the need to fill their heads with as much knowledge as possible. Tombar often directed his conversation towards Mala, who listened intently and appeared to retain knowledge easily. Jet had a short attention span but when the conversation turned to danger or adventure he listened carefully. Stryker caught the general gist of the conversation but was more interested in Tombar's wild stories and he was happy to let Jet and Mala make the majority of the decisions.

It was the evening of day twenty seven when the S.S.Hauraz finally anchored two miles out to sea off Lima, Peru, and waited for a vacancy to dock the gigantic vessel. Early the next morning a harbour-master was placed aboard the ship to navigate it safely into dock eleven. The water rats began to congregate near the shorelines as the tugs pushed the large ship against the wharf. They waited anxiously to descend the thick hessian ropes and run rampant in the port city. The geckos thought it wise to give the rats first preference and waited patiently for their turn to disembark.

Tombar approached the patient geckos.

"I want you to have this." He took a ring from beneath his fur coat and handed it to Mala.

"What is it?"

"It's a wish ring. There are only two wishes left from the original three, so use them wisely."

"Wow. Can we wish for anything?"

"Almost anything. It will not give you material riches or destroy a living thing."

"So what's the use?" Jet said impatiently.

"You will use it Jet! It will be for a greater purpose than that," explained Tombar.

Jet was silent as Tombar's profound words took seed.

Mala, Jet and Stryker bid farewell to old Tombar and promised to pass on his regards to Scully when they returned to Sydney. Then, with a mixture of excitement and apprehension, the three geckos touched land on their first visit to a new continent.

# 9. The Hazards of Lima

The geckos raced across the open ground of the docks and onto a street corner. After crossing the street they were confronted with a large embankment that led to the seaside suburb of Miraflores. A winding stone pathway led up the hundred metre escarpment, a journey that took the best part of thirty minutes and was a considerable drain on their energy resources. The walk and the scorching Peruvian sun forced the tired geckos to rest at the top of the hill and admire the stunning vista. Below them, a pier jutted out into the Pacific Ocean and people were surfing off the stony beach. Others were walking casually along it's promenade and enjoying the view, much like the three geckos.

"South America's very chaotic," Jet noted.

"Maybe, but this is only part of South America. There will be much more diversity than this. Tombar told us we would be exploring mountains, jungles and maybe even deserts. There is so much more to experience on this adventure. This is only our first city and I don't advise we stay too long," replied Mala.

They wandered along the rounded cobblestones that made up the short scenic wall.

"Hola my friends," came a cheerful sound out of the grass.

The gecko's normal instincts forced them to dart for cover.

"Amigos, it is I, Juan Antonio Fernandez, the most beautiful grasshopper in all of South America."

Out of the long grass hopped a large grasshopper. It's body was sleek and powerful and the natural striations of purple and yellow gave an indication of agility and speed.

"What do you think… am I not beautiful?"

"Yeah, whatever you reckon." Who have we got here? Jet thought.

The grasshopper turned and stared into the reflective metallic surface of a car, licked his stick-like front leg and brushed back his antennas as if he was doing his hair. Happy with his efforts, the grasshopper flicked his head and refocused on the amused geckos.

Stryker had brought one of his rounded fingers up to this mouth and pretended to vomit at the grotesque display of conceit.

"I am here to offer my services as a guide to my city; for a small price that is."

"But we have nothing to offer you," Mala said innocently.

"But you do, that jewelled dagger on your back will be worthy payment for the pleasure of my company."

Mala and Stryker stared at the dagger strapped to Jet's back and the jewel started to change from green to a dull red. The jewel indicated danger and they soon realised that the smooth talking grasshopper was not a trustworthy creature.

Stryker stared into Jet's eyes, then nodded towards the warning signs emitted from the *Dagger of Danger*. Jet picked up on Stryker's gesture and changed his demeanour towards the grasshopper. This was the second time it had changed colour, the first time had gone unnoticed, just before Sir Typhoid was about to strike a fatal blow.

"We only want directions to the centre of Lima," stated Jet.

"I will escort you the whole way," replied the grasshopper.

"No thank you." Jet was trying to be polite and ward off the grasshopper.

The fast-talking grasshopper's smile disappeared and in a nasty tone he threatened, "Give me the dagger and I will let you leave Miraflores unscathed." He whistled and seven other grasshoppers appeared from amongst the grass. Each one was sleek and dangerous.

"Let me repeat myself, give me the dagger and *WE* will let you leave."

Jet could see politeness was not working.

"I see you are not used to bargaining like we South Americans. It works like this…I set a price…you bargain lower…we deliberate…and eventually we compromise. My compromise to you… I will let you walk away without a broken leg."

Jet did not like the bargaining process the grasshopper had set and decided it was better to draw the dagger from it's sheath. This considerably increased his bargaining power, much to the annoyance of the grasshopper.

Juan, the Grasshopper approached Jet confidently. Jet tensed his muscles, and then swung the dagger in a full arc, slicing off one of Juan's antennae.

"Look what you have done. You have tainted my beauty," screamed Juan.

"Come any closer and you will loose more than that next time," retorted Jet.

Mala and Stryker were standing directly behind Jet.

"Make a wish Mala. Wish him gone," begged Stryker.

"Remember, the ring won't destroy a living thing. We'll have to leave it to Jet."

Juan approached a second time with added arrogance in his stride.

Jet did not hesitate. He swung the dagger with all his might to ward off the aggressive grasshopper.

*Swish.*

As he swung an arc of light emerged from the blade and the power it projected swept all the grasshoppers from their feet and flattened the surrounding grass.

Juan collapsed on the ground and his stylish appearance soon became a tangle of limbs. His evil associates staggered back into the bushes, hitting trees and tripping on roots. Juan wept where he lay, then propped himself up onto his shaky legs and stumbled off.

Jet was still shocked at the scene that had just unfolded and stared at the dagger. It was more powerful than it's stainless steel blade portrayed. It truly was a dagger against danger. The geckos regrouped and slowly retreated making sure not to turn their backs to their enemies.

"That was excellent buddy," exclaimed Stryker.

"That was very courageous Jet," reinforced Mala.

Jet blushed at the praise but quietly shook from head to tail at the experience. He was glad that it had happened as his confidence was boosted. He did not fully realise that this was a blessing, as it would prepare him for the adventures that lay ahead.

Up ahead was a tourist information centre or *tourista de information.* Two people were queued at the counter as the confident geckos crept under the wall and over to a large desk. They hid directly below the desk until the tour guide appeared to be deep in conversation about restaurants and the nightlife on offer in the city. The agile trio crawled onto the desk and rummaged through the maps until they found some that were useful to them. Jet kept point guard, Stryker watched the rear and Mala searched for more maps.

"A map of the city, one of South America and a bus timetable," she busily said to herself.

The contented geckos retreated off the table, under the door, and found a quiet corner near the cobblestone wall. Mala studied the map of Lima.

"We need to get to the central bus station in Lima and a taxi appears to be our best option." They were silent as they contemplated the next stage of their journey.

"We don't have to leave Lima so fast. Scully mentioned a place near the Church de San Francisco. We can stay a few days, adapt to the flow of life and get our bearings," Jet said excitedly.

"I thought you would want to leave this city immediately after what we've just been through with that sleazy grasshopper," Mala said with concern.

"I want to find the Sacred Gecko as much as any of us but I also want to have some fun on the way. Life's not only about the destination, it's about the journey. The incident with the grasshoppers wasn't the best start, but look at this place… we can have fun here." Jet smiled at Mala. "A little Latin music, some balmy nights, we'll wander the streets and even take in some of the sights. What do you think Stryker?"

"I'd like to stay a couple of days, the stories Scully and Tombar told of Lima were exciting. I want to see more," Stryker agreed.

Mala relented and they headed for the Hotel Espana.

A taxi came to a halt near the tourist office and a human couple wanted to go to the Plaza Del Armas.

"That's here in central Lima," Mala pointed at the map. "Quick, jump onto the back of that taxi."

The apprehensive geckos scurried onto the bumper bar at the rear of the taxi and leaned back to enjoy the free ride. They expected a relaxed ride but ended up with a 'hold on or get squashed' adventure. The local taxi drivers held the misguided opinion that they are driving dodgem cars at an amusement park. Every ten seconds the car would swerve wildly into a new lane or veer off down a ramp onto another crowded road. The Pollution Control Commission would be appalled at the smoke clouds billowing from the car's muffler. Most transport authorities would condemn some of the local buses as being nothing more than scrap metal. Still, in this city of approximately seven million people, life goes on.

After half an hour of bone shattering jolts the geckos disembarked at Plaza De Armas.

"What's this? It's a huge roundabout!" Jet answered his own question.

"It says here that the plaza was formed to commemorate the battles in which Peru has fought and to remember those Peruvians who died. That large bronze statue is a soldier on a horse and represents bravery," Mala informed the others.

"I think the pigeons should be more considerate, that guy on the horse looks like he has a bad case of dandruff," laughed Jet.

"Hey Jet they should make a statue for you. It would represent 'Gecko bravery' for kicking that Peruvian grasshopper's rear end," stated Stryker.

The Plaza de Armas was about one hundred metres across, with uniformly shaped garden beds and wooden benches for sitting. They would need to pass through three such plazas before they reached the Hotel Espana. It was only one in the afternoon, so they decided to walk. The Fresco architecture, large ornately carved doors and colourful walls made the city come alive. They completed the distance in just over one hour and with every step Mala came to appreciate Lima even more.

The Hotel Espana was a large, cheap hotel crowded with backpackers from every corner of the globe. It was a wild place where the humans dressed for comfort, not appearance. Mala and Stryker were apprehensive about going into a human habitat but Jet was becoming more curious about humans every day. They slid under the large wooden door and crept in behind the dark stairwell. It was reasonable accommodation and already had an ample supply of bugs living there.

"Let's rest up today and venture out tomorrow," suggested Jet.

All were in agreement, except the hotel inhabitants. As the night got later, the music got rowdier and the place became a hive of activity. Maybe humans are mostly nocturnal, Jet observed, but that went against all that he had seen within the large concrete hives that the humans inhabited back in Sydney. They appeared to be day creatures, but Jet wondered if maybe they came in during the day to sleep in the huge concrete towers of the city, and then ventured out each night to find food and a mate. Jet thought about this momentarily and then drifted off into deep sleep, the first one on stable land for almost a month.

# 10. The Catacombs of Death

Jet, Mala and Stryker awoke to the chiming bells in the church tower next door. It was still early, so they climbed the stairwell to the rooftop garden and fed on some of the local bugs. There was a touch of chilli spice in all the bugs; something that they would have to get used to over the coming months in South America.

The geckos basked in the morning sun before they returned to their stairwell home. They were going to travel light that day but Jet refused to leave the treasure map and dagger. They peered out into the street and were instantly surprised by the flock of ravens circling the tall steeples of the Church of San Francisco. The raven's mystical formation resembled vultures at a fresh kill.

They crossed the road to the church entrance.

"The first tours of the morning depart at nine am," Mala announced.

It was still only eight thirty am, so they crawled under the large Baroque doors and scampered across the ornate entrance. There were many magnificent paintings of the patron saints of Peru hanging on the high walls. As they wandered Mala would read the dialogue aloud. She was fascinated by the history but soon realised that Jet and Stryker were not really interested.

At the end of one room, stairs descended into the semi-darkness. They squinted and could see the outline of a large room, which had been carved into the bedrock of the church. Stryker and Jet were excited, but Mala was cautious.

"Wow, this looks creepy, doesn't it Stryker?" questioned Jet.

"The *Dagger of Danger* is still green so let's go and have a look." Stryker now had complete faith in the dagger's power.

The walls were damp and slippery, and what they thought was a single room turned out to be a maze of three separate passages all of which led deeper underground. There was a strange smell in the air but the room had no ventilation so they thought it was just stale air.

Jet pointed his finger at each door in turn "eenie meenie minie moe…" before he got halfway through the rhyme a shadow appeared in the door to the room on the left. It was the smallest of the three entrances but still quite large for geckos.

Jet approached the entrance as the gigantic shadow covered the entire doorway. The shadow had a central body and arms going off in all directions.

Jet was startled and leapt backwards onto Stryker's foot. He reacted immediately and pushed Jet further forward. Jet tumbled over the edge of the doorway and into a pit.

"*Ahhhhhhhh*"

He landed in a curled up shape on the ground. The dagger lay near his back feet and the map had rolled into the corner of the pit.

Above him stared a monstrous, hairy spider that was centrally positioned in a one metre wide web. The spider peered down at the prospect of breakfast. Jet had not analysed his adversary, and did not know whether he was safe as he stuck to the far wall.

"Hola Clumsy," the spider joked in a rather entrancing female voice.

"Hi!" Jet pushed off the wall and locked his attention on the spider.

The spider was not as big as they had initially thought. The light globe behind the web had caused the spider's medium size to be greatly magnified.

"What do you think of all your new friends?" Jesca the spider asked.

The spider knew Jet was too busy studying her to realise he had landed in a pit of one hundred and fifty human sculls. Jet turned to find he had leant up against the nasal cavity of a skull and had recently pushed off the eye socket of another in order to stand up.

"*Yuuukkkkkk.*"

Stryker and Mala peered down at Jet's dangerous predicament but were unable to help.

"What the…?" Stryker was speechless.

Mala just squirmed as she took in the ghastly sight.

"They're harmless. They have been here for hundreds of years," informed the spider.

Her words did not comfort him. He lay in a pit of human remains, beneath a church that had ravens circling it's steeple and he had a large spider above him who may decide that he'd be her breakfast. It all fitted together now... this would be the worst day of Jet's life. The spider could see the terror in their little faces and tried to relax the situation.

"I'm Jesca, a Peruvian Orb Weaving Spider and don't worry... I only eat insects. Does that put your mind at ease?"

"What is... what is... this place?" Jet stammered.

"It's an historic church burial ground which was once used to bury the nobility of Lima. After a ceremony in the church, the body was taken below into these catacombs, placed in a shallow grave and covered in quick lime to promote decay. There are over seventy thousand bodies buried in this place."

"Why would you want to live here?" Jet was inquisitive and a little more comforted. "It's creepier than Stryker's personality." He looked up and frowned at his friend who had pushed him down into this pit.

"Many tourists visit here, they drag with them fresh insects from the surface. The insects are blinded by the darkness and fly straight into my web. Not unlike what happened to you, but I think you would be a bit tough on my palate," explained Jesca.

She had warmed to the new geckos.

"How about I show you round? You look like tourists who could do with a hand."

Jet looked at the *Dagger of Danger* and the crystal remained green. It had only worked once to his satisfaction and Jet was still unable to put his entire trust in the colourful stone.

"Yes please, but I need a minute to recover and get out of here."

Jesca spun fresh web onto the wall of the pit and created a perfectly shaped, but sticky, ladder onto which Jet climbed.

Jesca crept from her web and showed the geckos around the catacombs. Some rooms contained only leg bones (femurs), other had just arm bones (humerus), and ironically the most interesting formation of all was the circular pattern of sculls into which Jet had landed.

"Where are you from my little friends?" enquired Jesca.

"We're from Sydney, Australia," Mala answered.

"I met someone from Sydney a year or so back, he also was the adventuresome type," Jesca reminisced.

"Was it a gecko?" Stryker was curious.

"Yes, but the name eludes me."

"Was it Sam?" Jet cut in.

"I really can't remember, but he was off to Bolivia and I gave him my sister's address in La Paz."

"Hey, that's where we are heading. What's it like?" asked Stryker.

"I have never been. I have a sister there, I send her messages when I can but that is hard to do. Why do you want to go to Bolivia?"

"We're on a quest to find the lost Land of the Geckos. It's situated in the Bolivian Amazon and we have to catch a bus from La Paz to get there. The dagger is for safety". Jet twisted his head and squinted his eyes. "What are you doing tomorrow?"

"Why?" Jesca inquired.

"We plan to catch a bus to La Paz at ten tomorrow morning, would you like to come with us?" Jet had a very convincing nature.

"Well I haven't seen my sister in some time but I will have to think about it."

"Please come with us. It will be nice to have another female along." Mala poked her tongue out at Jet and Stryker and giggled.

"I'll tell you what, if I decide to come, I'll meet you at the bus depot just before ten."

Jesca returned to her web at eight fifty five am, ready for the first wave of tourists and hopefully some breakfast. She bid the three geckos farewell and 'Feliz viage', which translates to 'happy travels' in English. All three geckos hoped Jesca would travel with them. They retraced their steps to the main entrance and out into the warmer sunshine. High above the ravens still circled the sharp steeple and a shiver went down the geckos' backs as they recalled all the skeletons below.

One kilometre down the road a crowd had gathered. The geckos went to investigate. There was a grand parade to signify the changing of the guard at the President's House. The humans had restricted access and stood behind a large metal fence to watch and photograph the neatly dressed regiment. The guards' costumes were very traditional and their overly exaggerated goosesteps amused the geckos but the machine guns they carried were a very real sign of the unrest that occurs in many South American countries.

The inquisitive geckos explored three more churches that day. Even through their apathy, the male geckos came to appreciate the history of this diversely populated country. Mala educated the boys as much as possible but by mid-afternoon their brains were full and they headed back to the Hotel Espana.

"Let's catch one of the crowded buses, my feet are sore!" Mala said wearily. "Look for Church de San Francisco bus and we're home".

Within five minutes, a small packed bus approached.

"Let's get on the front for a change then at least we will be able to see the trouble we're getting into," Mala suggested.

They had become bolder in their pursuits as they mellowed to the lifestyle of Lima. The front bumper bar on the bus had rusted from the salt spray and was hung loosely on two rattling bolts.

"Bonus, check this out!" Stryker yelled.

The front grill of the bus was a treasure trove of freshly killed insects ready to be eaten. Stryker called it 'Meals on Wheels' and a large smile remained plastered on his face as he munched happily on the bugs.

The three geckos were feeding away on their succulent, chilli-flavoured morsels when a traffic jam appeared ahead. They held tight as the bus lurched to a stop.

'HOOOOONNNNKKK, HONK, HONK'.

The startled geckos clasped their ears as the sound resonated into the core of their stunned bodies. The air horn on the bus came to life and nearly deafened the trio. It appeared all South Americans loved their car horns, and the louder the better. Stryker, being a very practical fellow, quickly ducked under the hood and bit through the horn wire. The Peruvian driver was infuriated when he realised that he could no longer vent his frustration using the noise of the horn. Jet and Mala clapped at Stryker's return and all three resumed their insect feast.

"That was fun, I'll have to remember to do that next time," laughed Stryker.

When they arrived back at the Hotel Espana the tired geckos spread out the maps and planned how they would cross from Lima to La Paz.

A bus left at ten in the morning everyday for the twenty hour journey to Puno, but here they would have to change buses and countries. They decided that tonight would be their last night in Lima and not to explore the nightlife would be a missed opportunity. Tomorrow they would have to leave for La Paz.

That night they waited outside the hotel door for a group of energetic backpackers. At nine thirty a disorderly foursome appeared and hailed a taxi. Their mannerisms were comical to the geckos and they appeared to be going out for a fun time. The backpackers jumped in the dilapidated taxi and yelled in unison *'Pizza Street here we come'*. The taxi ride at night still scared the geckos even though they had chosen the safer option of the rear bumper bar. The cars on the road came so close that Stryker tried to reach out to touch one but was dazzled by it's light before he could reach it.

It took half an hour before they arrived at the renowned Pizza Street; a well-lit promenade full of restaurants and loud Latin music. To stay safe, the geckos crawled up the walls and viewed the festivities from above. Every now and then they descended the wall to feed on some leftover morsels of food. They tried the chilli seafood pizza, Ceviche or raw fish with lemon juice and a strange fried steak and onion dish named Lomo Saltado. Mala found a drink called Guarana, an energy drink that is made from berries in the Brazilian rainforest. After a quick drink of Guarana the night changed and all three geckos became hyperactive. This was the first time the geckos had drunk this caffeine-type liquid. Jet felt light-headed and ready for anything, Stryker could not stop dancing to the Latin music and Mala just giggled a lot. They ended up dancing on the ceiling of various clubs in Pizza Street, allowing the Latino beat to infiltrate their souls and control their rhythm. Stryker lost his footing once, landing in a plate of sticky cheese nachos, but managed to eat his way out and be back dancing on the roof within five minutes. They found the rowdy backpackers again in the early morning hours and crept onto the back of their taxi bound for Hotel Espana. Lima had left it's mark on the geckos' minds and all three wanted to return on their way home from Bolivia.

# 11. The Trouble with the Shining Path

It was after eight in the morning and the three geckos still slept soundly. Stryker was the first to wake and quickly roused the others. They were slow and drowsy in their movements in the morning and only just able to direct themselves to a bus terminal owned by the Ormena Company, the largest bus company in Lima. They made it on time and were grateful to Stryker for waking them as this was the only bus that left for Puno each day. This would climb the Andean Mountains to heights over five thousand metres where the scenery could only be described as breathtaking.

When they spotted the Ormena bus they were shocked at the decaying metal body of this vintage coach. The roof racks were already half full as a man stacked an array of items ranging from the sublime to the ridiculous. There was anything and everything from beds to rice bags, backpacks to armchairs, and even a sheep was strapped to the roof. The squat Peruvians waited patiently for the bus to leave while Jet, Mala and Stryker looked anxiously for a place to spend their journey. It would be cold in the high Andean mountains so they should be inside the bus but it was crowded with humans so that would be impossible. Jet saw a plastic covered mattress being passed onto the roof and pointed it out to the others.

"When it gets cold we can retreat into the mattress for warmth, and when it's nice we can cruise on the roof and be guaranteed to pick up some freshly squashed bugs."

Stryker was happy. "I can't think of anything better, let's go."

They were so busy they had forgotten about Jesca until they saw a spider creep along the rafters of the bus terminal.

"Jesca," Mala pointed.

Jesca turned and shot a long spindle of web that joined the terminal rafters to the bus roof, and then slid along it like she was on a flying fox.

"Jesca, I'm so happy to see you," smiled Mala.

Jet was pleased. "Glad to have you as part of the gang."

"Well I thought it was about time I went to visit my sister. She keeps telling me about the Witch Markets. Apparently the food there is excellent" Jesca stated.

"Witch Markets, as in witches, warlocks and spells?" Stryker asked.

"Yes I suppose so. That's what she told me anyway."

"And she lives there?" Stryker could not keep off the topic.

"Yes," Jesca confirmed.

"You live in a church surrounded by human bones and you want to visit a sister that lives with witches?"

"Yes. I never thought of it like that; pretty strange don't you think? You never know I may eat one of you yet," Jesca laughed.

The first few hours of the trip were spent navigating out of Lima's vast urban sprawl and onto the road leading east into the mountains. First stop; La Orayo. The bus would then turn south along the Andean highlands to Hauncayo, Cuzco and finally Puno. Once out of the city the three geckos went up to the front of the bus for some food, Jesca stayed behind and spun a small web to catch her own fresh insects.

The adventurers also decided to visit the black and white Peruvian sheep they had seen loaded on the bus earlier. The sheep had a rope around its neck and was tied directly to the metal rungs. The rope was taut so the sheep had to crouch slightly and splay its legs in order to remain upright while the bus went around the corners. Jet, Stryker and Mala felt sorry for the poor restrained animal and went up to have a conversation.

"Hello there, we can't help but notice that you're in a bit of a bad predicament. We thought we might be able to help you out" Jet stated.

"I know, but I'm fine. I appreciate your concern," said the sheep in a slow, deep voice. "Where are you little ones travelling to?"

"We're heading to the lost Land of the Geckos in the Bolivian Amazon," Jet stated proudly.

"The Amazon is a big place. I hope you find what you're looking for," replied the sheep.

"Thank you. So do we. We have a map." Jet patted the map on his back.

"The Amazon is an amazing place. You will find your Gruber tool will come in very handy in the jungle."

"What Gruber tool?"

"Don't tell me you travelled all this way without a Gruber tool."

"What is a Gruber tool?"

The sheep was surprised at the innocent geckos. "A Gruber tool? Everyone knows you don't go into the Amazon without a Gruber tool!"

"What does it do?" Mala questioned.

"Can you reach in behind my front ear? There's one tucked in my wool."

Jet reached over and pulled out a small metal rod with a sharp hook on the end. There were words on the shaft - 'No mas peligro'.

"That says *'No more danger'*. I was told it will direct me to safety, but I'm not really sure how it works. The only thing I was told was to keep it dry or it will reverse it's function," warned the sheep.

"I'm not sure about this," Mala said cautiously.

"You can have it. I got it from a travelling monkey but I never intended to go to the jungle. Wool and jungle plants don't mix. I like the grassy plains."

"Thanks," said Jet.

"Just remember to keep it dry. The monkey was very specific about that," reinforced the sheep.

"Sure. Is there anything we can do in return?"

"Yeah. Just loosen the rope a little."

Stryker loosened the rope. They bid farewell to the sheep and went back to see Jesca with their new Gruber tool.

"What did you say it was?" Jesca asked.

"A Gruber tool. Have you heard of one?" Jet inquired.

"No." Jesca was intrigued.

"I'm suspicious but Jet wants to keep it," Mala replied.

"It may help us out more than you know." Jet slid the Gruber tool beside the *Dagger of Danger*. They were both secured to his back by the leather strap.

"We should do something nice for the sheep," Mala insisted.

Stryker desperately wanted to use the ring. "Let's use the ring and give it freedom."

"We shouldn't waste the powers of the ring," Jet said protectively. Mala was compassionate.

"Don't be selfish Jet, do you think the sheep will see it as a waste?"

Jet succumbed to Mala's charm. "No. That's a nice idea."

They went back up the front of the bus to talk to the sheep.

"Where would you like to go?" Mala inquired.

Just then the bus was passing a lush green mountain field.

The sheep was wistful. "How about you just let me off here."

Mala held the ring up and made her wish. The sheep vanished and magically appeared in the field nearby.

"Wow," shrieked Stryker.

The sheep waved and the geckos were excited.

"Let's keep this safe and make the last wish something special," Jet advised.

They retreated back to Jesca and told her all about the ring's powers.

The hours went by quickly and the combination of the setting sun and a rise in elevation to over three thousand metres caused the temperature to cool considerably. Jet was about to doze off when the bus swerved wildly to avoid sharp metal spikes on the road. His body rolled inside the circular tube of the mattress and came to a halt in a pile of geckos and the tangled legs of Jesca. They peered out of the mattress and realised all six of the bus tyres were punctured.

"Who would have done that?" Stryker questioned.

Suddenly two four-wheel drives laden with guerrilla troops appeared from behind a small ridge.

A scream erupted within the bus. It appeared that the locals knew what was happening but unfortunately the geckos and Jesca did not.

The four-wheel drive vehicles were painted a camouflage green and aboard were six men and two women, similarly dressed. They had khaki uniforms, a red beret on their heads and a patch on their right shoulders unifying them as "The Shining Path". One of the women had a definite purpose in her stride and her uniform was all black.

Two subordinates entered the bus first securing the scene and then the leader made her way on board.

"I am Sebrina," began the athletic young Peruvian. "You have been detained by the Peruvian Shining Path (or Sendero Luminoso in Spanish).

We are dedicated to the creation of a classless society and wish to take all your belongings in order to fund our operations. If you decide to oppose us you will be dealt a severe lesson. Could you please all step off the bus and strip to your underwear?"

"What's happening?" Jet was curious.

"Shhh," commanded Mala softly touching his foot to reassure him he would find out in a minute.

The moments passed.

"OK," began Mala, "the bus has been captured by a Latino Guerrilla group called the Shining Path who have ordered everyone off the bus and are threatening violence."

"Oh great, and I wanted to sleep in this morning," Stryker complained sarcastically. "That would have been much better than this."

"Let's sneak off the other side," Mala suggested.

A moment later a round of bullets tore into the exterior shell of the bus, encouraging the passengers to hasten their departure and to demonstrate the seriousness of the group. One of the bullets exited the bus just centimetres from Mala's head causing her to freeze. Jesca reacted swiftly and shot a web from the bus to a nearby tree. She swung into the tree and quickly formed a web shaped like a safety net.

Jesca directed the geckos towards her newly created web. "Quick, jump over here."

Jet grabbed Mala's hand and was airborne before she came out of her shock. Stryker was not far behind and all three geckos landed safely in the rudimentary web.

"This is really sticky," Stryker complained.

"What do you expect, I normally eat whatever lands in my webs," Jesca gave Stryker a wicked grin.

Stryker grimaced.

The passengers began to strip their outer clothes in the cool mountain air, while two of the Shining Path members drove the bus off the road. The bus rattled loudly while being driven on it's metal wheel hubs. Once out of sight another band of troops would begin to strip the vehicle for their rewards.

Once the passengers were down to their underwear the Shining Path guerrillas searched for money belts and purses. Having recovered what they wanted they left the group stranded, leapt into their four-wheel drive vehicles and raced off into the mountainous terrain. The group was lucky not to have casualties.

"What do we do now?" Stryker muttered as he looked at the panicked locals who were just coming to terms with the terrible predicament they were in.

"There will be other cars along this road to pick up the locals. We only travelled about one hour from the last small town but I don't think we need to backtrack. Let's bed down here for the night and wait for tomorrow's bus."

"I don't have a better idea," Mala agreed.

Jet, Stryker and Mala found the decaying hollow of a tree branch and curled up together for the night. Jesca spun her web over the top of the hollow to protect her friends from unknown predators in the night and also settled into a deep sleep.

# 12. The Lick of the Llama

The sunrise was spectacular as it greeted the Andean Mountains and awoke the four small creatures to a new day. The sky was a magnificent red, typical of South America with it's dry desert landscapes. Trees are not abundant on the high Andean plains but the breathtaking scenery and the small colourful patches of Polylepsi woodland made for excellent viewing.

After breakfast, which was conveniently caught in Jesca's overnight web, Jet and Stryker decided to explore their immediate surroundings. Mala was happy to remain behind to enjoy Jesca's female companionship and the two talked quietly.

Jet and Stryker decided that they would not wander far, keeping within sight of the tree in which Mala and Jesca were chatting. The surrounding slopes were rocky with a collection of thick grassy mounds and stunted trees. They had not gone far before they mounted a large boulder and peered down into a flock of long necked sheep with red ear tags.

"They're the weirdest sheep I have ever seen," Jet stated.

"Are you sure they are sheep?" Stryker queried.

"What would you call them?" retorted Jet.

"It's like a giraffe was crossed with a sheep and then decorated like a Christmas tree."

They both laughed at the thought. All the animals were too busy grazing on the stunted grass to notice the small geckos on the rock.

"Hey check this out......BAA, BAA, BAA," Jet yelled at the giant sheep.

The large animals looked up and started towards the two geckos.

Jet and Stryker stared in horror as the animals moved towards them.

"Now look what you've done!"

They ducked below the rock edge hoping their small size would obscure them from view and waited for about ten minutes.

"Do you think it's clear?" Stryker panted.

"You look Stryker, Jet challenged.

"We'll both look. Ready, on the count of three. One, two…."

"Is that on three or after three?" Stryker queried.

"On three. Ready, one, two, three."

They poked their heads over the top of the rock and stared face to face at one of the monster sheep.

"AHHHHHHHH."

The creature had lowered its long fluffy neck over the top of the rock and licked Stryker's back. A trail of saliva stuck to Stryker's scaly skin and he squirmed in disgust.

"What was that for?"

"I just wanted to see what you tasted like before I ate you," smirked the monster sheep, as it winked at it's five friends.

Jet and Stryker ran as fast as their little legs would take them. In the background they heard the snickering of the five monster sheep that had not bothered to chase them.

They ran back to the tree and told Jesca and Mala about the attack from the hideous monsters.

"They're llamas Jet," Jesca informed.

"Not giraffe sheep?" Jet was still worried.

"No, their wool is very fine to touch and extremely warm. They're pretty harmless."

"But they were going to eat us, they told us so."

"They're herbivores and only eat the tussock grasses and leaves. They were playing a joke on you."

Mala laughed, this would be a good story to tell the other bridge geckos once she returned home. Jet and Stryker could only just raise a smile as they realised they had been on the wrong end of someone else's prank.

The rest of the day they all stayed near the tree, they had no energy and no desire to deal with any more new encounters that day.

The sun was low in the sky so they decided to get organised before the next bus arrived on it's way to Puno.

Mala broke the slumbered silence, "Hey, I just had a thought, the bus won't stop here, not like yesterday. It will be going at full speed down the road."

They had failed to think of this. There was no bus stop where they were and if anything the driver would be going faster in this area to avoid any further trouble.

"I'm sure the Shining Path will not pull off the same manoeuvre two days in a row in the same place," Jet decided.

Everyone was silent as this mental picture was being put into perspective.

"Hmmmmmmmm."

"OK, let's think. We know how high the bus is from the safety net Jesca made yesterday, right". They nodded. "So if we get Jesca to make a web that will cross the entire road, then we hang from the middle, and jump onto the roof again." Jet clapped his hands as if the problem was solved. Stryker and Mala knew the outcome last time this had happened from the Harbour Bridge. Stryker was almost squashed to the front windscreen and Jet had almost rolled off the back of the bus.

"But I'm too heavy," Stryker said shyly, "and jumping out of a sticky web onto a bus travelling at sixty kilometres per hour is not my idea of fun."

Jesca came up with an idea but was unsure and set to work without informing the others of her plan.

Over the next hour she busily spun webs in all directions. The webs criss-crossed the road in what must have been hundreds of metres of intertwined spider's web. Later she concentrated on more intricate work in the centre of the web, moving in restricted zones and being very thorough. Jet, Stryker and Mala were intensely curious but did not disturb her exhausting work. The sun was not far off the horizon and the next bus would be here soon.

"Taaa Daaa," Jesca stood in the middle of the web and bowed at the geckos.

"What is it Jesca?" Mala questioned.

Suddenly the bus appeared over the far horizon, its headlights shining brightly down the distant road. There was no time to answer.

Jesca scurried for the edge of her web as the bus approached.

One hundred metres away and the bus was still travelling at about sixty kilometres per hour, the gravel spraying from it's wheels as it swept around the bend. A large plume of dust rose behind the bus as it thundered down the dirt road. The geckos' hopes of catching the bus were sinking with every passing metre.

The bus was fifty metres away and there was still no sign of it stopping. They felt the vibration from the earth as the bus bounced along the corrugated surface.

A frown of disappointment formed on the geckos' foreheads as the bus approached. Another night in the mountains was not what they had hoped for but it appeared to be their destiny.

Thirty metres from the web the bus driver's face transformed, his eyes shone and he slammed on the brakes. The bus swerved and skidded to a halt less than a metre from the web. The passengers were shocked and shaken as they stared out of the windows, fear of the Shining Path foremost in their minds. Jet, Mala, Stryker and Jesca scuttled along the ground and up the side of the bus heading for the roof.

The bus driver pushed the heavy lever that opened the squeaking door and approached the web. He stared at its fibrous makeup and shook his head. Bewildered, he brushed the side of the web and reassured himself that humans had not made it. He shook his head again and returned to the bus. He apologised to the passengers and then drove right through the middle of Jesca's sign.

The geckos had watched all this and looked at Jesca in amazement. From this angle they could read the large letters that had been woven into the web and covered the entire roadway, but were unable to decipher the Spanish meaning.

"What did it say Jesca. What is 'despacio omnibus cerrado?'"

Jesca laughed, "It said *slowdown bus stop*."

They all laughed. Jesca was a very clever spider. They then settled in for the night ahead.

It was early morning when the bus arrived in a town named Cuzco. The town was beautiful, with intricately carved stonewalls and churches. Jesca informed them that the Incas had lived in this area long before the Spanish invasion in the early sixteenth century. The Inca

Empire had existed for a few centuries, having an intelligence and architectural advancement similar to that of the Ancient Egyptians.

The bus remained in Cuzco for only one hour and then it was off to Puno. The latter journey was in daylight and the geckos just hung out on the rooftop, ate some bugs and absorbed the stunning scenery. They experienced a two-hour delay in Puno as they crossed the border from Peru into Bolivia, then onto a new bus destined for La Paz, the capital of Bolivia.

At the end of this second day of travelling the mountains appeared larger and more formidable. The terrain was barren and the elevation was greater than four thousand metres above sea level. The bus climbed slowly out of a small depression in the high Andean plains and ahead the geckos could see a dome of light that radiated out of the valley.

"That must be La Paz. See here," said Mala pointing to the map of South America.

This was now the first time a symbol from Scully's treasure map had been able to be located. They were within the context of the treasure map and the excitement was electric. Jet's thoughts turned to his father, and the hope and longing had now intensified significantly since he was first given the map by Scully.

"You must be excited Jesca. How long has it been since you saw your sister?" Mala asked.

"Two years. I hope she is still there."

The bus approached the rim of the valley and the geckos looked down to see a myriad of houses that climbed out of the valley floor and up the surrounding slopes. The city of La Paz followed the river line through the valley and the surrounding hills were very steep. The lights from the small houses shone over the earthy red roofs of the one's below them and there was a distinct pattern from the intersecting roads that contoured the hillsides. La Paz was before them and now the map would truly come into play.

# 13. The Witch Markets of La Paz

The adventurous geckos and their spider companion approached a large central bus terminal on the upper slope of the valley.

"I don't have a map for La Paz yet. Look for one of those Tourista places again," Mala ordered.

Throughout South America the tourist stands are located at all the vantage points to help the weary and lost traveller.

"Over there!" Stryker pointed.

"No, that says 'Taco' Stryker, which is a food stall."

"That's even better and they both start with T."

"I'll have to teach you two to read one day," Mala shook her head.

"Over there," Jesca pointed and sure enough it was a *toursita de information*.

As in Lima, the geckos and Jesca crept under the door of the tourist office. Jet and Stryker stood watch and Jesca and Mala found two maps, one of La Paz and another for Bolivia. They ran under the nearest bus and studied the map out of sight of the humans.

Mala ran her fingers over the map "Witch Market, Witch market. Here it is, the Witch Market. OK, it's too far to walk but if we catch a bus to Avenida de Santa Cruz it will only be a short walk from there."

"Let me just check again. Are we sure we want to stay in a Witch Market? There must be a thousand other safer places to stay," Stryker remarked.

"Nothing personal but we appear to invite trouble on ourselves sometimes."

They all knew Stryker had a point but Jesca's sister lived in the Witch Markets and they could not disappoint Jesca.

"Come on. Jesca said it would be fun. What could possibly go wrong?" Jet encouraged.

They walked outside the terminal gate to catch a local bus.

Many local buses passed along the outside of the larger terminal and it was not long before they had found the one they wanted. They jumped on the front bumper bar and Stryker quickly darted out of sight.

"Where's he gone?" asked Jesca.

"He's our handy man; he disconnects the driver's horn so that we don't lose our hearing on the trip. It's easy for the driver to fix it again later," answered Jet.

Just then Stryker returned with a confident smirk of satisfaction, slapped his hands together and said "Well, we're just about to make another South American bus driver very unhappy."

At Avenida de Santa Cruz the four small creatures disembarked and crawled up the nearest wall for safety and a good view.

"What does a witch look like?" Stryker was worried.

The geckos had never seen one before but they had heard that they were mean, nasty and had warts. Jesca had relayed stories from her sister about the potions that the witches make. They were not the same witches as those depicted in western fairy tales.

"I don't see any witches with black pointy hats and brooms, do you Stryker?" Jet joked.

There were many people all around and strange aromatic smells wafted through the air.

"I don't know. This place gives me the heebie geebies," Stryker added.

They proceeded down the small street staying high on the wall. Small laneways ran off Avenida de Santa Cruz and suddenly they realized they were in witch country. They rounded the wall and were engulfed in a waft of smoke that temporarily blinded them. Below them was a buxom woman sitting on a wooden stool. Her colourful dress billowed out from her waist in a mixture of purple, black and red. Her hair was tied in a bun under a small bowler hat and her face was withered and wrinkled. Two bowls hung by her side occasionally emitting clouds of strong herbal aromas. However, it was the table ornaments at her stall that caught everyone's attention.

On the table were dried llamas decorated in tinsel and surrounded by bags of herb and potions. There must have been about ten different dried llamas, all purposefully decorated with varied bags at their feet.

Along the shadowed lanes many such women sat giving an eerie feeling to the entire area.

"I told you this would be creepy," Stryker stated.

"That potion is to stop voodoo curses, that one's for eternal life and that strange orange one is for exorcism." Jesca pointed out from her knowledge of South American culture.

"So, because I have an orange back means I need an exorcism?" Stryker concluded with much anxiety.

They crept along the lane wall trying to remain inconspicuous. Halfway along one lady caught their movement and peered at them. She had deep brown eyes and so many furrows in her face it looked like an empty hessian sack. "Beunos Dias my little lovelies. I think I have found some fresh lizards gizzards," the old lady snarled. "I could make a wonderful potion for blindness with those large beady eyes."

She picked up a broom lying behind her chair and made a swipe at the wall.

Jet's dagger shone red as they fled the scene. The old lady was rather nimble for her age and shuffled along the creepy alley taking the occasional swipe in the gecko's direction. One was a near miss and the wind from the broom head almost swept Mala off the wall. Luckily Stryker was there to grab her.

There was a small gap that divided the stonework of the two buildings. They rushed ahead and took a sharp right turn. The lady stood at the entrance and made two more swipes into the crevasse before giving up and going back to her stall.

The crevasse was only four metres deep and was blocked by a rather large and uninhabited spider's web.

Jesca's eyes lit up and she ran for the web "Lucia! Lucia!"

"Wait Jesca, what if that spider is not friendly?"

"It is my sister's web, I can tell!"

Jet, Mala and Stryker were sceptical, they had seen many spiders on the bridge and all the webs looked alike.

"It must be a distinct type of web from Jesca's species of spider." Mala added.

Jesca turned around. "No silly. You have watched me make a web. It is often a labour of love and a caring spider is like any artist when they make a creation. It takes time and effort to make such perfection. When anyone creates a piece of art like this they sign it." Jesca pointed to the lower right corner of the web and sure enough it had Lucia's signature.

"Does every spider do this?" Jet was curious.

"Of course, we all have a spot of vanity. Look more closely next time you see a web, I guarantee it will have the artist's signature in the lower right corner."

They shook their heads in amazement.

"You learn something new every day!" Stryker nodded his head.

Lucia heard the commotion and appeared from behind a sandstone crack in the wall. She was shocked and emotional as she greeted her sister in a tangled hug of legs and legs and more legs.

"*Hola me hermana.*"

"Hello my sister."

"It has been a long time," Lucia sighed, "I am so glad to see you."

Lucia looked over her sister's shoulder at the curious geckos that stared at her.

Jesca turned to the geckos, "May I introduce to you Mala, Stryker and Jet. They are from Sydney, Australia."

"You have come a long way my friends. May I welcome you to my home? *Mi casa tu casa.* Which in Spanish means *my house is your house*." Lucia's voice was warm and friendly.

"Thank you." Mala was comforted.

"If it wasn't for these geckos I probably wouldn't be here so soon," Jesca remarked.

"You are a long way from home my little friends," Lucia smiled.

"They are on a quest to the Bolivian Amazon in search of *Tierra Del Gecko*," explained Jesca.

"Really." Lucia's tone had changed and this worried the geckos.

"Why?" asked Jesca.

"Arr, *Tierra Del Gecko*. I haven't heard that mentioned for quite a while."

"That other gecko I sent your way arrived, I gather?"

"Yes. Sam stayed about a week and then left for Rurrenabaque. He also told me about *Tierra Del Gecko*."

"Sam. Did you say Sam?" Jet interrupted.

"Yes. Sam, a nice gecko, full of spirit and bravado."

"How long ago was this?"

"Probably eight months ago. I have not heard from him since. I told him to call in on the way back."

"He's my Dad," Jet said proudly.

"Ah yes. I can see it in your eyes. The eyes are the gateway to the soul".

The three geckos were one step closer to the answer and Jet was encouraged by Lucia's words.

"Tell me more about him Lucia. Was he well? Excited? Tell me everything."

"I will tell you Jet but I will tell you all later. Right now I want you to make yourselves comfortable. I'll duck out and get us some food and tomorrow I will show you around La Paz."

"Watch out for the broom lady, she swings a mean stroke."

"Which one, there are about twenty of them," Lucia chuckled.

Lucia returned with an array of juicy dinner treats from the local markets.

They sat up late into the night and discussed La Paz, life and more often than not, the quest for *Tierra Del Gecko*.

The next day Lucia showed them around La Paz. They hitched rides on buses, taxis and even a wooden horse-drawn cart. Their first stop was *Mercado Negro*, or the black market area. This is a haven where the thieves and illegal importers sell their goods to the public, all for cash of course.

"Hey, that guy just stole someone's wallet!" Stryker pointed.

"This is the black market my friend, legality is not really an issue here," explained Lucia.

They wandered through the markets, the colourful stalls and the winding streets. They had lunch at the top of a church steeple. Jesca and Lucia cast webs between the spires that quickly trapped a variety of insects for them to eat. As Jesca had pointed out previously, they both signed their webs in the lower right hand corner.

By late afternoon they retreated to the Witch Markets, avoided the broom-swiping old ladies and returned to the dark sandstone wall of Lucia's home.

"It gets a bit cold around here at night," shivered Mala.

"Yes it does. The city is actually three thousand six hundred metres above sea level, the highest inhabited capital city in the world," informed Lucia.

"Is all of Bolivia like this?" asked Mala who was not used to cold weather. "We have a long trip ahead and we may need some jackets."

"I can arrange some jackets, a spider friend of mine is an excellent tailor and with eight legs and your small sizes we could have something for you by tomorrow night. For tonight I will get some extra bedding cloth from the local material shops. That will keep you warm." Lucia was very accommodating. "Anyway, soon you will be heading to Rurrenabaque. That's in the Amazon Basin, thick with rainforest, hot and humid. You won't need jackets there".

"Now that's a relief," Mala was small and got cold quickly.

"What can you tell us about Rurrenabaque?" Stryker asked.

"I haven't been there," replied Lucia. "Those who are fortunate enough to return normally talk of wild animals and dangerous conditions. Up in the jungle they tell me there are deadly piranha fish, ferocious jaguars, pack-hunting wild pigs, poisonous tarantula spiders and enormous anaconda snakes."

"Snakes. I hate snakes!" Stryker squirmed.

"These are not just normal snakes; these are huge," Lucia added.

Lucia stopped and looked at each of the geckos in turn as she gauged their reaction. Jet looked excited, Stryker looked apprehensive and Mala squinted in deep thought.

"Go on," Jet said excitedly.

"You have to catch a bus on one of the world's most deadly roads. They have nicknamed it *'The Death Road of Bolivia'*. Apparently twenty vehicles plummet off it's steep and rugged edges each year. The worst section is a sixty kilometre long, single lane, dirt road. This one section of road descends from a five thousand metre snow-capped mountain pass to one thousand metres and into the thick and humid

Amazonian rainforest. The road is often undercut by water erosion, there are no guard rails on the edges and the road has vertical drops ranging from fifty to three hundred metres. Buses have been known to plummet into the rocky chasms never to be seen again."

Even Jet took a large gulp of air at the exhaustive description of their next bus ride. Being attacked by the Shining Path now appeared to be a minor distraction in comparison to this 'Death Road of Bolivia'.

"Just one question," Jet inquired.

"Yes Jet?"

"What do anacondas eat?"

"Anything they want…The Green Anaconda grows to about five metres. However, some of the larger species have recorded lengths of eight to nine metres and about thirty centimetres across their middle. They are like one long, powerful muscle. Anacondas will wrap around their prey, slowly constrict the oxygen flow and eventually suffocate them to death. They then disengage their front jaw and engulf their prey in one, long, rhythmic swallow."

"Wow!" Stryker was astonished.

"I wouldn't worry too much, you're not exactly a tempting meal, and you're too small. They normally feed on deer, pigs, fish and caiman. The caiman is a creature that looks like a small crocodile."

"Thanks very much. I'm sure to have pleasant dreams tonight," Stryker squirmed.

Lucia changed the conversation to more logistical matters concerning transport and timing. Once they were all happy with the fundamentals they split and Jesca retired to chat with her sister.

The geckos discussed their next stage of the expedition in a private section of the sandstone crevasse.

"So, what do you think?" Jet prodded. Jet was excited, but the others were silent for some time.

Mala broke the silence. "How did you talk me into this trip again?" she frowned.

"Yeah Jet. I've heard the term undying friendship for your mates, but I never thought the saying was based on fact," Stryker added.

Jet ignored their doubts and unrolled the treasure map of 'Tierra Del Gecko'.

"Well, we finally made it to a place on the map." Jet pointed at La Paz showing he had improved his map reading skills.

He paused to let Mala and Stryker absorb the map and the excitement it held. "We can't go back from here," he added.

"We know that Jet… but the road ahead is dangerous. We'll have to take it slowly and plan well."

"That's what I always do," Jet said defensively.

"Yeah right," Stryker and Mala laughed sarcastically.

"What's this fire around the anaconda's cave, I didn't notice that before?" Mala pointed at the map.

"I thought they were red bushes but I think you're right Mala that is fire." After a brief pause Jet added, "It may just be for visual effect on the map but I'm sure we'll find out soon enough."

All three were silent for about a minute as they stared at the map.

Mala softened her voice. "Your Dad is probably not far away now and we all know this is driving you forward, but let's just be careful. OK?"

Mala sympathized with Jet but was concerned that he may act emotionally and not logically, as they plodded forward on the quest.

"Sure…. I still can't believe we have got this close. Only a couple of months ago we had never been off the Harbour Bridge. Now we're about to find a golden gecko that is protected by a giant anaconda."

"Yeah… I can't believe it either," Stryker said dryly.

The next day the three geckos did some more planning. They went around the markets and collected enough cloth to make backpacks for Mala and Stryker. Jet would still carry the *Dagger of Danger*, gruber tool and the treasure map, however they wanted to carry some weapons and implements to repel the anaconda if needed. They would need all the help they could get. It would be an unfair match between the three ten centimetre long geckos and an anaconda that would be nine hundred centimetres long!

# 14. The Death Road of Bolivia

On the fourth day Jet, Mala and Stryker decided it was time to leave La Paz and catch the *'Death Road'* bus. Jesca would stay with Lucia until they returned and then she would catch the bus back to Lima with them.

One bus a day leaves La Paz for Rurrenabaque and it takes eighteen hours on a good trip but many days on a slow trip. They bid farewell to Lucia and Jesca, loaded their backpacks, avoided the broom-sweeping witches and boarded a local bus. This bus took them to a larger bus terminal where they searched for a coach to Rurrenabaque. When they saw the bus a feeling of terror swept across the trios' faces. It was about half the size of a real coach and had 'Rurre' written on the front. Rurre was the local's name for Rurrenabaque.

"You have to be kidding me, we're not going on that thing," said Stryker.

"I think we may have to, but at least now I know why it's called the *Death Road*," exclaimed Jet.

The bus looked like it had already fallen off the road a number of times.

"Come on, let's go have a look." Jet led the way towards the bus.

The bus was medium sized with a podgy nose and a large rear end. It had a blue bonnet, multi-coloured sides and large worn tyres. The roof racks were piled high with what appeared to be the entire contents of a household.

Scrambling up the side of the bus the geckos found a gap on the roof and nestled between four corn bags; it seemed comfortable and protected. The engine roared and a cloud of smoke billowed from the rear of the vehicle, blanketing the nearby commuters with it's noxious plume. The driver eventually found first gear and the sound of grinding metal pierced the surrounding air as the small multi-coloured bus lumbered down the road. It took half an hour to climb out of the La Paz valley and a further hour before they reached the pinnacle of the five thousand metre Coroico Pass. On the crest of the pass the view was spectacular but now it was time to descend the *Death Road* section of Bolivia.

Jet, Stryker and Mala lay flat on the front of the bus. If something was going to happen on this *Death Road*, they may as well witness the event. The pleasant two-way tar road had now given way to a one-lane, two-way dirt road. Only one road rule applied, the vehicle travelling uphill had the right of way. Any vehicle going down would have to reverse back up the hill and onto the corners to allow the other vehicles to pass. Stryker sat the furthest left and had the best vantage point to observe the two hundred metre vertical drop on his side of the road. They had not driven too far before they met their first oncoming vehicle. It was a heavily laden fruit truck and it had the 'right of way'. The road was not wide enough for the both vehicles. The bus driver had to cautiously reverse up the winding road until he found a bend where the truck could pass.

"Where is the driver going?… HOLD ON, I think he's going over the edge," Mala yelled. All three geckos clung to the roof, every hairy suction-like follicle on their feet gripping tightly. The bus came to a sudden halt. It's long rear section dangled mid-air over the steep cliff face. All eyes peered down the sheer drop. The human faces inside the bus had whitened with fear. The truck passed and the bus lurched forward to recommence it's downward journey.

"I hope we don't meet many more of those," Mala said in relief.

"This is crazy, my heart beat just tripled," Stryker exclaimed.

"Hey look at that," Stryker pointed at the beaten remains of a bus of similar colour that was strapped to a couple of trees on the edge of the road.

"It hasn't got any windows and look at the dents in the sides," Mala commented.

"That looks like it's been hauled out of the gully. Look at all the broken tree stumps and bus parts in the valley," observed Jet.

They all stared at the beaten bus, thankful that it was not their own.

It wasn't long before the bus reached the base of the valley and the windswept five thousand metre pass gave way to lush tropical rainforest.

Stryker wriggled, "I need to take this backpack off Jet, these two metal canisters are digging into my spine."

The three Geckos retreated back to the corn bags and unloaded their gear.

Stryker had two pressurised gas canisters in his backpack used for making home soft drinks and Mala had sections of rope, some rags and pieces of mirror in hers.

"The backpacks will be safe here. Let's relax a while," suggested Jet.

Mala and Stryker slept protected from the wind. Jet curled his body but slept restlessly as the thoughts of his father preoccupied his mind. He awoke in the early hours of the morning, climbed to the top of the highest corn bag and watched the scenery that surrounded him. The silence of the pre-dawn was relaxing. He felt a movement at his side, Mala had come to join him.

"Are you alright Jet?" asked Mala.

"Yes." Jet's voice was not convincing. "I know my father is here. I can feel it inside."

"He may be Jet, we can only hope." She rested her foot on his and they watched the spectacular sunrise in silence.

The clouds that had settled low overnight were rising from between the tree canopy. The birds and monkeys began to chatter in the pre-dawn excitement. The music of the rainforest dwellers peaked just after dawn as the hot humid conditions of the Amazon River basin wafted it's thick scent.

"This really is a paradise." Mala commented as she looked at the brightly coloured flowers, inter-weaving vines and vibrant bird life.

"It certainly puts the cities to shame," Jet replied.

# 15. The Bolivian Amazon

It was another six hours before the bus finally drove into Rurrenbaque. They arrived at midday, thankful to be rescued from the harsh midday sun. The town was smaller than expected, a jigsaw puzzle of thatched roofed houses and rough dirt streets. The town was built on the Rio Beni, a tributary of the mighty Amazon River.

The bus was immediately surrounded by some of the local community who had come to meet their relatives or attract tourists to their small hotels. The geckos were amused by the commotion and did not notice the large colourful bird that landed on the back of the bus.

"*Hola Amigos. Como estas?*" greeted the bird.

The shocked geckos leapt for the protection of the corn bags. This bird was gigantic and had a forty centimetre long orange beak. It's beak was as long as the bird was tall. It's back was a mass of yellow feathers that fused into the black plumage of it's chest.

"*No problema amigos. Yo no peligrosa,*" it apologized.

"I'm sorry we don't speak Spanish," Mala yelled from behind the corn bag.

The large bird's eyes lit up. "Why you no explain? I am no dangerous," the colourful bird smiled.

"I say *hello friends, how are you?* I am the mayor of the animal community of Rurrenabaque and I come to welcome any new visitors on this bus everyday. My name is Pablo and I am a Toco Toucan."

The tentative geckos eyed the dagger on Jet's back but it remained green. The Toucan saw this strange movement and looked at the *Dagger of Danger*.

"You do not intend to try to hurt me, do you?" asked Pablo the Toucan.

The three geckos looked back at Pablo in shock.

"Oh no... we're peaceful and only carry the dagger in case of danger," Jet calmed Pablo.

"Well that's a relief," Pablo said jovially.

"I am Jet, this is Mala and this is Stryker"

"We have a tree house in town called 'The Bopping Beni'. There's music, food and drink. I would be most honoured if you could visit as my personal guests."

"Thank you Pablo. How will we find it?" Mala asked coyly.

"It's in the top of the largest tree beside the boat ramp. You just have to follow the wonderful Latin music."

Pablo smiled as he danced around on the top of the bus. "Do you need help with accommodation?"

"No… We'll be…."

Mala cut Jet off in mid-sentence "Yes that would be most helpful."

"Well climb aboard."

Pablo bent down beside the corn bags and the geckos retrieved their backpacks and climbed on his back. They had been taught that every bird is dangerous but now they realised they had been stereotyping.

Pablo took three steps and then soared into the thick humid air.

"Here's an aerial view of the town, it will help you get your bearings. There's the Rio Beni, there's the party tree by the boat ramp and there's the main street."

Jet looked at Mala and could not believe the smile on her face. She was having the time of her life. It truly was a feeling of complete freedom. They swooped low and then climbed high, learning more about Rurre as they went. They could see Pablo had pride in his hometown and instantly liked his personality. Ten minutes went by before Pablo landed beside an abandoned boathouse.

"I know lizards like to be cool and damp so this should do fine". He lifted one wing and pointed down the riverfront. "The tree house is three hundred metres that way, along the shore. Just watch out for the snakes!"

"Thank you Pablo, we'll see you tonight," Jet said enthusiastically.

Pablo then flew off across the river.

The boathouse was rustic inside, just large enough to fit a small fishing boat. The wooden planks were slightly decayed and the thatched roof allowed rays of sunshine to pierce it's canopy. Pablo was right, it was damper and cooler than outside and would make a perfect base from which to launch their expedition. They searched around their new home for a place to rest. In the corner they found the remnants of the last guest who had lived here. Someone had left some colourful rags, a small magnifying glass and an unmade bed. The wall had hundreds of notches carved into them like a prison calendar and a candle stump tucked into a crevasse.

"Jet, Mala, get over here."

"What is it Stryker?" queried Jet.

"Does this say what I think it says?" Stryker asked.

Letters were carved into the boatshed's frame.

Mala read aloud, "I will find *Tierra Del Gecko - SAM*."

The letters were old and mould had grown in the carved cracks. They knew they were on the right track.

That afternoon they rested and studied the map.

"Do we tell Pablo about the map?" Stryker asked.

"No, I don't think we should. Well, not just yet. I also don't want him to know I'm Sam's son. He may not even know Sam. Tonight we just tell him we're geckos from Australia and see where that leads us."

They refocused on the treasure map and Jet plotted their future course.

"Here's the Rio Beni, we need to get up the river to here". He pointed to the map, "This is the Rio Tuichi, but the distances on the map don't look accurate."

"It's so close now Jet." Stryker clenched his fist and flexed his muscular arm in excitement.

After about an hour they re-rolled the map and lazed around, ready for the night ahead.

"Pablo said this way," Stryker pointed.

"Can't you just smell the steamy nights?" Mala sighed.

"I can't believe how many insects live in the rainforest. This is like a smorgasbord." Stryker licked his lips.

"So we agree this is a good place to be?" Mala asked.

They wandered along the river's edge careful to stay out of the lights that beamed down from the human houses. The tree ahead had a faint glow in it's high branches.

The geckos had climbed about six metres up the tree and could feel the music vibrating throughout the trunk.

"Careful of that wire," Stryker warned, "It's probably electricity for the Bopping Beni Club."

They were now twenty metres above the ground and a large platform blocked their view of the open sky. Jet knocked on the hatch door and a wooden shutter slid back.

"Can I help you?" asked an animal in a deep reverberating tone.

"Pablo, a large orange-beaked Toucan, invited us here tonight," Jet stated.

"Pablo?"

"Yes, Pablo."

"Well why didn't you say so!"

Seconds later the door was opened by a giant sloth. His paisley waistcoat and strong muscular arms were daunting, but the music and bright lights were very welcoming.

"Wow, what a cool place." Stryker was obviously impressed.

Above them appeared a multi-levelled clubhouse built into the tree's branches. The main timber floor was about three metres long by four metres wide. A bar made of bamboo was situated at one end, there was a thatched roof overhead and cane furniture was evenly spread for the patron's convenience. A radio was playing on a makeshift stand and music radiated from all four corners of the room. The music had a throbbing Latin American dance beat that soaked into the inner core of the geckos' souls. The atmosphere was laid back and the mix of animals varied.

A large group of Leaf Cutter Ants sat in one corner chattering away, some Howler Monkeys swung their bodies on the dance floor, a Scarlet Macaw chatted with a Blue Azure over wing dynamics and some Neon Blue Morpho Butterflies perched happily on a nearby branch.

Pablo saw them enter and politely left his tapir friend to make them welcome.

"Hola, my friends."

"Hola Pablo," returned Mala.

"Ah, you learn Spanish well, my pretty one."

Mala blushed.

"Come have a drink with me."

"We don't have money Pablo."

"Ah, in the animal kingdom you do not need money, you either collect what you need or borrow it from the humans," he said waving his wing around. "We have borrowed all this." Then he whispered. "But we have not told them yet." Pablo chuckled.

"Four jungle delight sodas thanks Renaldo."

Renaldo was a Howler Monkey and barman. He used his extraordinary energy to mix a wild fruit concoction in a bar shaker. He placed the shaker in his tail and swung it wildly until it became a frothy yellow-green punch.

"Cheers," Pablo saluted.

"Cheers," chorused the geckos.

"To *Tierra Del Gecko*, may someone please find it," Pablo announced.

The thirsty geckos had already started to drink and simultaneously choked on Pablo's words.

"To where?" Jet gulped.

"*Tierra Del Gecko* or Land of the Geckos, whatever you prefer." Pablo was toying with his words.

"But…" Jet stammered.

"But what? You underestimate me my friends, I have lived here for many a year and you are not the first to search for *Tierra Del Gecko*."

"You knew all along," confirmed Mala.

"You are not well disguised. Australian accents and you are geckos… no?"

"Well, yes, but." Jet was embarrassed that they had been so obvious.

"But nothing my friend, I will help you in any way I can. I have helped those who have come before you, but by the time they reach Rurrenabaque none of them have retained their map, as you have."

"You saw that?" Again Jet was dumbfounded by his indiscreetness.

"Of course. I know a gecko who will be very interested to meet you, but alas, he is up in the jungle searching for the ancient Gecko City."

"Who might that be?" Jet could not help himself.

"It is Senor Sam."

The gecko's faces beamed with excitement.

"You seem pleased my friend. Do you know him?" Pablo smirked.

"Yes, he is my father. He has been missing for a year from our Sydney colony. Most geckos assume that he is dead, but I have never given up hope. It was not until three months ago that we met a rat who had a copy of my father's map. We set out to search for the ancient *Tierra Del Gecko* and to find out if my father is still alive."

"Sam is getting close to solving the mystery. I have noticed a twinkling in his eye and we all know that some day soon he would be victorious in his quest. The problem is, he is now one week overdue from his latest expedition and the locals are starting to get worried." Pablo explained.

"Where was he searching?" Mala asked.

"In an area that's west of the Rio Tuichi, full of rugged rocky peaks."

"Do you know exactly where?"

Pablo looked Jet in the eye. "I was the one who dropped him there. I have been out there many times over the last few days but he has not returned to our rendezvous point."

"Is that the map on your back?"

"Yes," Jet said defensively.

"May I have a look?" inquired Pablo.

In the corner of the bar there was a vacant table where the geckos and Pablo sat. Jet sat in the farthest corner facing the bar as he wanted to keep an eye on the other patrons. He unrolled the map but was constantly glancing around.

"Ah, this fits together now." Pablo concentrated hard. "Your father had his map stolen in La Paz by a witch. He told me she dislodged it with a wild swipe from her broom."

The geckos felt remorse for Sam but grinned at the thought of the witch with the swinging broom. Jet looked up from the map many times but no one in the room appeared suspicious. Jet did not realise that the *Dagger of Danger* was burning red…. danger was near.

"Your father then drew another map from memory but he missed out on some vital information, such as the cave shaped like a key hole and the fire around the snake." Pablo studied the map intensely.

"I said that was fire around the snake," Stryker interrupted.

Pablo continued, "Sam searched east of the Rio Tuichi for many months, all the time in the wrong spot. Your father is in the right place now, but I fear for his life."

"Why?" Jet retaliated.

"There is a legend in these parts about a giant anaconda that has fire dripping from it's fangs." Pablo paused to build the suspense. "I have never believed it and I don't know anyone who has seen it. But here, see these words on the map, 'Serpentaria de Feugo', they confirm my worst fears."

Pablo was silent, a worried expression crept across his face.

"What do they mean Pablo?" Jet wanted to know.

He got up from his seat and paced the floor.

"It translates to *Serpent of Fire*. If this is true…" he sighed and looked at the table, "If it is true, then we will most certainly have a battle on our hands."

"We have to save Sam!" Pablo was concerned.

The glow from the dagger strengthened.

High above the tree house there were two green tree snakes that busily watched the entire conversation.

"It seems like our master will have more pests disturbing him soon," hissed one of the snakes.

"We must get word to Voltar. I think he will want to know that three more geckos will be visiting him soon," hissed the other snake.

They slithered off down the tree trunk.

A black crow was waiting for them.

"Tell Voltar that three more geckos will be there within the week. Also warn him that Pablo the Mayor is involved again," hissed the snake.

The dark crow spread it's intense wingspan and flew silently into the night.

"When can we leave Pablo?" Jet asked.

"Tomorrow, if the weather is fine."

"Tomorrow it is!"

"And if it is not?" Mala asked cautiously.

"I cannot fly in the rain with three passengers on my back, we will have to wait. The weather controls our life in the jungle but it is a wonderful place to live."

They rose from their seats and Jet felt the warmth in his back. He glanced quickly at the dagger but the snakes had left and the crystal had reverted to green. He was not concerned, it must be the nerves and the hot climate he concluded.

Jet lifted his glass of jungle delight, "To our mission and our destiny!"

"To your father's health," replied Pablo.

Once they had finished their drinks the geckos retraced their steps back to the old boathouse and fell into a deep sleep.

# 16. The Serpent of Fire

They woke to the sound of torrential rain beating onto the small tin boathouse. Pablo had arrived early. His feathers were damp from the rain and the water dripped through the cracks in the boathouse roof.

"We can not fly today," he said apologetically, "but don't be discouraged my friends, there is meant to be a change in the weather tomorrow."

"Thanks Pablo," Jet replied, but you could see he was impatient and irritable.

"I'll fly around at the same time tomorrow."

Pablo stared into Jet's eyes and could see the pain. "Jet. ...Nothing can be done today and I have good feelings about our future."

"Thanks Pablo," Mala changed the mood, "I would like to wander about Rurrenabaque and see what this tropical town has to offer."

Pablo smiled at this interest in his beloved town. "Visit the Mercado my friends, at lunch time it teems with people and a great variety of food."

"Fooood," Stryker smiled.

They agreed to go out for lunch but were to spend the morning studying the map of *Tierra Del Gecko*. The anxious geckos tried to commit as much of the map to memory as possible. This would lessen the mistakes once trouble began, and they had a feeling it would.

As lunch approached Stryker's stomach began to rumble and grotesque noises came from it's inner cavity. Jet had to laugh and this lightened the mood considerably. Jet was sympathetic.

"Come on then Stryker... I guess it's time for lunch at the markets."

The street outside the boathouse had turned to mud and there were no footpaths in this small town. Torrents of water cascaded off the thatched roofs with enough force to sweep the small-legged geckos into the canal.

They had to be careful, but luckily the market was only two hundred metres from the boat shed. It was the slowest two hundred metres they had ever travelled.

The *Mercado* building was one of the few concrete structures in town, and with it's bland grey walls it did not add any beauty to this sleepy township. Inside the two-storey, hollowed out building there was a hive of activity. The small vegetable, fruit and meat markets on the lower level were doing excellent business due to the wet conditions outside.

"Upstairs smells better," Stryker stated as he charged up the side of the concrete walls.

The upstairs area housed the food court and delicious aromas swept throughout the whole Marcado. From their aerial view the tiny reptiles could see many ladies cooking frantically at their stalls, all the while trying to lure new customers. People could sit near a stall of their choice and be handed the one meal that was being served that day.

Stryker went off on his own tangent and said, "That fish looks nice."

"Meet us back here with your meal Stryker." Jet wanted everyone to stay together but Stryker's stomach was a dominant force.

"What about you Mala? The chicken and rice look good."

Mala and Jet feasted on what was left at the stall and eventually the trio of content geckos returned to the boathouse.

"That chilli spice is hot but I think I am getting used to it," Stryker said with a smile, but you could tell from his watery eyes that the chilli still burnt his lips and mouth.

That night passed slowly and anticipation of the day ahead kept each of the geckos awake. Jet could not stop his restlessness and proceeded to double-check the backpacks. The gas cylinders were fine, ropes okay, rags still there and the pieces of mirror were still unbroken. Jet had added some aluminium foil to the collection, something that may act as a fire barrier.

The thought of a giant anaconda snake with fire dripping from it's fangs was enough to keep anyone awake. They had been told by many to fear snakes due to their unpredictable and cunning behaviour. How could a snake have been born with fire dripping from it's fangs? Wouldn't it have burnt itself when young? Does it have any brothers or sisters? Why does it have the key to *Tierra Del Gecko*? All these questions remained unanswered in the geckos' heads as they tried unsuccessfully to sleep.

The early rays of sunshine beamed through the thatched roof and brought a smile to the red-eyed geckos. The weather was sunny, not a cloud in the sky. Jet was admiring the wonderful weather when he heard a rustle in the grass and saw something slither away. They were being watched. His first guess was a snake, but it was small and discreet. The giant anaconda could not know about them already! Jet decided not to tell the others.

When Pablo arrived half an hour later the geckos had eaten breakfast and were ready to venture into the jungle.

*"Buenos Dias,"* Pablo turned his head and looked at Mala, "which for you, my pretty little Spanish student, means good morning."

Mala smiled and repeated Pablo's words, "Buenos Dias Pablo."

It was now Pablo's turn to smile.

"OK, OK... let's be off before school starts." Jet said.

"You are every bit as eager as your father," Pablo said proudly.

Pablo squatted down and the three geckos climbed on his back again. Three steps later they left the ground and soared over the Rio Beni.

The Rio Beni was wide near Rurrenbaque and flowed slowly. Pablo flew upstream and the sides of the river soon narrowed and the once calm river was now a mixture of fast flowing currents and turbulent rapids. Many dug-out canoes would navigate this river and it was only their long narrow shapes and powerful outboard motors that allowed them to pierce the swirling rapids.

"How far is it Pablo?" asked Mala.

"About one hour my friend. We will follow the Rio Beni for half that time, then at the tributary we head up the Rio Tuichi."

"This is the way to get around Jet, much better than taxis and buses." Stryker was enjoying himself.

Mala had a constant smile and soaked up the view of this wild terrain.

Up ahead there was a fork in the river and Pablo veered right to follow the Rio Tuichi. The riverbank was jagged rock and the pictures in the map became more realistic.

A boulder almost blocked the entire river and Pablo turned right and followed a smaller stream inland. The terrain was made up of jagged rocky peaks that pierced through the thick inhospitable rainforest.

"See that large peak over there," Pablo pointed his beak. "That's where I was supposed to meet Sam a week ago."

"Let's fly around some more and look for the key hole cave and any sign of smoke from the serpent's fire," Jet suggested.

"Which direction?" Pablo asked.

"Hey, where's the Gruber tool?" Mala asked Jet. "Remember, it was meant to lead us out of danger, so wherever it points, we go in the opposite direction". Mala could see they did not understand.

"The Gruber tool points to safety." She waited till they nodded. "The giant anaconda will not be safe." They nodded again. "So whatever direction the Gruber tool tells us to go we fly the opposite direction and find the anaconda." They finally saw the light and smiled.

Jet got out the Gruber tool and laid it on Pablo's back. It swung in circles and finally came to a halt facing towards the river.

'Pablo, fly away from the river."

Pablo did as he was told and the three geckos peered into the deep forest below. It was hard to see into the darkness let alone find a cave. Then from a deep ravine up ahead a small puff of smoke rose through the canopy.

"Did you see that?" Stryker yelled.

Mala confirmed his sighting and passed the information on to Pablo.

"We can't land down there, it's too close to the cave and the jungle is too thick. Let's land on that rocky outcrop, it's an excellent point from which I can keep watch."

The rocky outcrop jutted out forty metres above the thick forest canopy and was only one hundred metres from where the smoke was sighted leaving the rainforest. Trying to peer into the dense canopy of the rainforest was impossible. Pablo would have to let the reluctant geckos travel on foot from here, a scary proposition.

The geckos decided to descend into the jungle canopy immediately and travel under the cover of the leaves. They had only gone twenty metres when another burst of smoke wafted before their eyes. The smoke had a foul odour as it drifted their way, a smell of evil trapped amongst thousands of leaves. Once below the canopy eighty percent of the light had filtered out and they had to rely on their large eyes and excellent vision to guide them.

"Down there," Mala pointed.

The outline to the cave entrance took shape and their heartbeats doubled.

The *Dagger of Danger* was burning red and they all knew they had found the right place.

Jet now took charge. "Ok let's stop here for five minutes and study our surroundings."

The minutes of silence felt like hours, but their patience was rewarded when the two anacondas that guarded the cave entrance, came outside to chat. Their bodies were long and thick and the geckos were stunned by their immense size. Both anacondas had stern faces and their tongues continually prodded the air trying to detect any scent of intruders.

The geckos stared at their adversaries trying to pick up any hint of personality or ability.

"Any suggestions?" Jet inquired.

'Yes. The boatshed at Rurrenabaque is looking really cosy right now," Stryker suggested.

"We can't go back, my Dad's probably in there," Jet pleaded.

A period of silence followed as the geckos thought about their situation.

"There has to be another way in, a crack in the rock, an air vent; lets search for one of those first," Mala suggested.

They scoured the upper surface of the rocks above the cave, all the time being careful not to make any noise. The rock was a slippery cobblestone, and they trod carefully. Suddenly the dagger sheath moved sideways and got caught on a rock. Jet was flung to the ground and while he scrambled to stop himself falling he dislodged a small rock. It felt like slow motion as the rock plummeted towards the cave entrance. The geckos froze. Jet rolled onto the dagger to conceal its bright red glow. The two anacondas slithered rapidly out of the cave and peered upwards. Their forked tongues whipped the air trying to pick up a scent. The wind was still and the geckos were lucky this time. The trio of geckos remained motionless and within five minutes the anacondas gave up and went back into the cave.

The geckos resumed their search for an opening into the cave.

"Here," said Stryker pointing to a crack in the rock from which a strange smell rose.

"That's not very large, I'll go have a look." The crack was long and narrow and it disappeared into the darkness.

Jet shuffled between the rocks and was soon lost from sight. He travelled at least five metres before a light source appeared before him. The crack widened revealing a large cave. Jet froze in shock at what he saw.

A ten metre long green anaconda laid before him, it's muscular body thirty centimetres across looked like a steel cable. It was coiled on a large flat circular rock in the centre of the cave. The rock was like a throne and the anaconda was it's master. The throne-like rock was surrounded on all sides by hot, bubbling tar pits and a stone bridge joined the throne to the rest of the cave. The anaconda was sleeping, but even in it's sleep, small droplets of clear fluid would run down it's fangs and drop like fireballs to the earth.

Wrapped in it's many coils was the shining gold statue of *Gecko de Oro* or *The Golden Gecko*. Jet stared open-mouthed at the beauty of the golden statue. It reflected the firelight which beamed to all corners of the cave. Stryker is not going to like this, thought Jet.

Jet was about to leave when a movement caught his eye. In the corner of the cavern there was a small cage built from rainforest timber. Jet stared at the cage and within it was a withered looking gecko with a fiery red tail. It was his Dad and a feeling of warmth crept through Jet's body. The snake was keeping Sam prisoner for some unknown reason. Was Sam going to be it's next meal? Was there something more sinister planned? Jet had to get back and tell the others.

Jet had been gone for about fifteen minutes and Mala and Stryker were beginning to worry. From deep in the crack they could see the glow from the dagger rising upwards. Jet's face was pale and the shock was evident.

Jet spoke slowly. "OK... this is no normal snake. Think of something from your wildest imagination and double it. It's ugly down there...but my Dad is there."

"That's wonderful news," Mala said excitedly. "Well the second part is wonderful news."

"He doesn't know I'm here but it was definitely him."

"You saw him?"

"Yes but he looked scared and weak," Jet spoke softly. "Here, let me draw you a map and get you orientated. We need to be ready before we go in."

Jet retrieved the treasure map and drew a picture of the cave on the back. They discussed the plan but needed to move fast. They would need to get into the cave and take the snake by surprise while it still slept. As long as the snake was asleep they knew they had an advantage.

They spent the next few minutes getting organised. Jet covered the dagger handle with cloth to prevent any undue attention from it's red glow. Stryker went to warn Pablo of a fast departure, and told him to lure the cave guards away from the cave mouth in fifteen minutes time. Mala attached ropes to the packs in order to lower them down the narrow crack. Once they had finished their individual tasks they returned and faced each other. Each placed a foot into the centre and gave each other a look of confidence and strength. The adventure was risky and they knew that they might not survive.

Mala and Jet went down the crack first and secured the backpacks that Stryker lowered into the cave. Mala could not believe what she saw. This was truly a serpent of terror. Stryker quickly followed and they all scurried for safety behind a rocky wall. Stryker's face was more shocked than Mala's. He had told Pablo to be a decoy and that they would wait until he lured the other two snakes away before they made their next move.

The minutes ticked away and a then large screeching sound came from the entrance of the cave.

"Did you tell him the giant anaconda was sleeping," Jet asked Stryker, "and we don't really want to wake it up?"

The screeching continued. "I think I forgot to mention that Jet." He bit his lip as the noise echoed throughout the cave.

The giant anaconda awoke, stretched his spine and looked around for the cause of the disturbance. It looked over at Sam with a strange smile. Sam was lying quietly in his cage and the dreadful noise was coming from outside.

"Quiet down out there or I'll eat you both," Voltar bellowed at his guards.

He looked over at Sam and hissed contently. Sam bore an excellent resemblance to the gold statue that the serpent seemed to prize above all else. Voltar may be dangerous but he appeared to be superstitious. The noise continued and Voltar slithered his large muscular body towards the entrance of the cave and commanded the smaller anacondas to chase Pablo away. They raced off subserviently leaving the cave entrance unprotected.

"Now," Jet commanded.

The trio split up, Jet headed for Sam's cage, while Mala and Stryker scampered for the golden statue. Voltar was busy at the entrance and did not realise the trouble that was unfolding within his domain. Jet reached the wooden cage and took Sam by surprise.

"Jet… is that you?" Sam thought he was hallucinating from lack of food and the heat of the cave.

"It's me Dad, I can't explain now, we have to move fast."

"It's so good to see you… but how on earth did you find me here?"

"I'll answer everything later." Jet did not have time for small talk. "Stand at the back of the cage!"

Jet drew the *Dagger of Danger* and slashed the vines holding the wooden cage in place. The front wall collapsed and Sam dashed out and hugged Jet.

Mala and Stryker had scampered across the bridge to the throne-like rock. "This looks heavy," Stryker frowned "Are you sure we need to bring this?"

"This is *Gecko De Oro*, we don't quite know the significance but it must be a clue to the secret of *Tierra Del Gecko*. We need this Styrker," Mala demanded "Lets tie it to your back and you can carry it."

Stryker stared at Mala but she was already retrieving the ropes from her backpack and did not notice. It would be a supreme effort but they could not think of any other way.

All was progressing well until Voltar turned around. He was already mad after being awoken from a deep sleep and now this. A piercing hiss echoed through the cave and droplets of fiery venom sprayed directly towards Stryker and Mala. Mala gathered two of the mirrors and deflected the brunt of the heat but this was only a quick fix to a larger problem.

"Go with them Dad," Jet prodded his father in Stryker and Mala's direction.

"But..."

"No buts, we'll talk later."

Sam was proud of his son's maturity but was afraid for his safety.

Jet quickly wrapped his body in aluminium foil, a desperate measure to protect himself from the fiery venom of Voltar. He grabbed one of the two gas cylinders and ran across the gap that divided Voltar from the other three geckos. His aim was to be a decoy and lure Voltar in his direction. The giant snake hesitated momentarily but preferred the more adventurous option and struck out in Jet's direction. Jet was still out of reach but the gap was closing fast. Voltar continued to chase Jet and the distance was now perilously close.

Voltar spoke for the first time. "What do you little vermin hope to achieve?" He hissed down at them. "I already knew that you were coming" he teased the geckos. "You showed Pablo the Toucan the map when you were in the Bopping Beni."

Jet was taken by surprise, had Pablo double-crossed them? Had he led them to Voltar's lair? What was happening?

Voltar quickly covered the ground that separated him from Jet. He struck again. This time his venom only narrowly missed Jet's side. Mala, Sam and Stryker crept along the far wall of the cave and headed for the entrance. Mala picked up the remaining backpack but the weight of the golden statue made their combined progress slow.

Voltar spat a barrage of fireballs in Jet's direction. He was able to avoid most of them. Three struck the aluminium foil that was wrapped around his body and burned him only slightly. A fourth fireball struck his unprotected front foot and this caused great pain. Jet hobbled and Voltar knew that the next strike would be fatal. Mala, Stryker and Sam stopped and watched Jet anxiously and saw the peril Jet was in. He had the aluminium foil wrapped around his body, the dagger on his back and he clung desperately onto one of the gas cylinders.

There was no hope left. Voltar was upon him. Jet could do no more. He relaxed his body and looked towards his gecko friends. His face showed little emotion but his eyes read deeply; a look that said 'goodbye'.

Voltar struck aggressively and engulfed Jet's body in one swift mouthful. With no remorse he turned, rattled his forked tongue and looked for the others. They were frozen and emotionally bankrupt. Tears welled in their eyes at their loss, and their bodies began to tremble as they were now in the same position.

Voltar coiled his body and opened his mouth wide in a theatrical display of terror. He loved the drama this was creating and the powerful rush was like adrenalin in his system. He kept the situation tense as he wanted to break the geckos' spirits before he swallowed them.

Jet had been swallowed whole and was being violently shaken around inside Voltar's stomach. As the anaconda's body rippled the stomach contents churned like a cake mixer. Gastric acid within Voltar's stomach burnt Jet's eyes as he tried to stabilise himself and find the gas cylinder. He got within two centremetres of the cylinder and Voltar moved again throwing him further down the digestive tract. Jet was again within reach of the gas cylinder and dived with all his effort. It's slimy metal cover began to slip from his grip, he had little energy left but applied what remained to holding onto the gas cylinder. Then as Voltar stopped momentarily, Jet drew the *Dagger of Danger* from his sheath and sent the dagger crashing into the mouth of the gas cylinder.

Suddenly Voltar's body contorted, his muscular mass began to expand. The gas cylinder released it's pressurised contents and the snake changed dimensions. A balloon like shape began to appear at his midriff as his body began to inflate. Voltar opened his mouth to relieve the pressure and Jet's body hurtled out in a rush of air. The air was mixed with bony debris, gastric fluid and the stench of burnt remains. Voltar's stomach contents reached the far corners of the cave and the three geckos had to avoid the flying particles. Voltar's body continued to expand as the contents of the gas cylinder were released. His eyes bulged in their sockets and he shrieked as his body ballooned further.

Jet wiped off the sticky contents from Voltar's stomach and yelled at the others "Ruuuunnnnn!"

They helped Stryker support the weight of *Gecko de Oro* and rushed for the main entrance. Before they could reach it an explosion occurred within the cave and fleshy pieces of anaconda came hurtling past their heads.

The daylight was bright on their sensitive eyes and their nerves were at breaking point. The fact that Voltar no longer existed allowed them to relax slightly. Stryker sat down and let out a large sigh as the solid earth took up the weight of the statue.

"I'm glad that's over," he added.

"Not quite yet my friend," Jet assured him.

They peered out in front of the cave and could see the two anaconda guards returning fast. Their bodies whipped loudly as they slithered like steam trains toward the cave. They had heard the explosion and hoped their master was not harmed. Pablo had led them deep into the rainforest and Jet had a renewed faith in his feathered friend.

"Where is the other gas cylinder?" Jet asked.

"Here," Mala fumbled with the backpack.

"Hang in there Stryker," Jet ordered him as he strapped the remaining gas cylinder to the opposite side of the statue.

"That's not funny Jet." Stryker's voice was concerned, "Do I look like a rocket?"

"No but a lot of hot air comes from your mouth sometimes."

How could Jet make jokes at this point in time, Stryker wondered?

Jet stopped smiling. "I think a temporary rocket ride will be better than another visit to an anaconda's stomach. What do you think?" Jet pointed at the two six metre long anacondas that motored towards the cave entrance.

"Houston to control… Space Shuttle is ready for take off," Stryker added nervously.

The gas cylinder was secured and Jet ordered Mala and Sam to intertwine their hands around Stryker's body… and hang on. Mala looked at the ring on her finger and decided this was worth a wish.

She closed her eyes and concentrated, "I hope we can get out of this safely."

Jet winked at her and smiled as he tied the remaining rope around his waist and connected it to the statue. He drew the *Dagger of Danger* and delivered a violent blow to the cylinder head. The gas erupted from the base of the cylinder with great power. Their feet became light on the ground and the statue wobbled as the pressure released from the cylinder increased. The anacondas were only twenty metres away and the seconds felt like hours. They finally lifted off the ground in a rush of energy. The four-gecko crew of the statue rocket hurtled towards the leafy canopy above.

They accelerated fast and turned their heads aside as the canopy leaves whipped their faces. The power produced a gravitational force on the geckos called G-force, which caused their faces to change shape slightly.

The gas cylinder had a thirty second life span and once it had burst through the rainforest canopy there would be a loss of thrust and power. The geckos felt the slowing of the upward force and were eager to stand on solid ground.

"We seem to be running out of power here Jet," Stryker said. "I don't suppose this statue has a parachute?"

"Pablo, where are you?" Jet yelled. This would be the test to see if Pablo was truly their friend and had not double crossed them and led them to Voltar.

"Is that your answer?' Sam chuckled in disbelief. "We're one hundred metres above the ground, strapped to a four kilogram gold weight and you want Pablo to rescue us?"

"Well...yes," Jet looked down and saw his foot was bleeding from Voltar's fire burn. The flow of adrenalin was too intense for him to worry about his pain. Pablo was their only hope.

They reached the pinnacle of their upward flight and for a brief second felt suspended in mid air. Gravity would soon take charge and they would hurtle back through the canopy to the waiting anacondas. This was not a pleasant thought.

Then, from out of the canopy their brightly coloured friend emerged. Pablo's wings flapped heavily as his sharp claws grappled at the golden crown of the statue. He had to work hard to keep the four geckos and statue airborne and only just managed to bring them down safely onto a rocky outcrop.

"We're safe, we made it and we have the statue of *Gecko de Oro*," Jet cheered triumphantly. "And I have my Dad back." He turned and smiled.

Sam and Jet hugged each other and the whole group joined in. They could feel the release of tension and the relief on their faces was intense.

"Pablo, you have to forgive me, I questioned your friendship in there. Voltar had me thinking that you were on his side. I'm sorry I doubted you," Jet apologised.

"You must be wary of those snakes, they can be very cunning." Pablo was very understanding. "You rest here', I'll fly back to Rurre and get some help."

"Are you disappointed Dad?" inquired Jet.

"Disappointed by what son?"

"That there was no *Tierra Del Gecko*, and only *Gecko de Oro*."

"Yes. A little." Sam sighed. "I was after the fabled land of the geckos but this statue only goes to prove that there is something more. However I did realise something whilst trapped in Voltar's cave. I realised I have all the treasure I need right here."

"Where?"

"Well, one of them is right here with me," Sam put an arm around Jet, "and the other, well, she lives on the north pylon of the Sydney Harbour Bridge. I don't need a map to find that treasure."

The four geckos sat on the rocks for many hours talking about home and what they would do when they returned. Jet's leg was bandaged with the remaining scraps of material and they waited patiently for Pablo's return.

# 17. The Mystery of Tierra Del Gecko

Hours later Pablo returned with three more toucans and a couple of azure parrots. They had a basket ready to carry *Gecko de Oro* and each of the exhausted geckos had their own bird on which to fly home.

That night a large party was held in their honour at the 'Bopping Beni Club'. This was the biggest party that Rurenabaque had ever seen. The centrepiece was *Gecko de Oro* and the town animals loved it. The toucans squawked loudly, monkeys leapt around the trees, butterflies flashed brightly across the room and the club was a sea of colour and excitement.

Stryker ordered a few Guarana drinks, like in Lima, and began his wild dancing style. He was having a fantastic time but accidentally knocked the statue against a tree branch. The statue struck the floor solidly.

Stryker turned to the crowd all embarrassed. "Sorry about that."

However the music had now stopped and all eyes were on the statue. The blow had unveiled a secret cavity in the base of the statue. The club members stared as the events unfolded. Sam, Jet and Mala rushed to the base of the golden statue. A key rolled out and they caught it before it skidded across the floor.

"What's this?" Jet examined the key. The handle was shaped like the head of a gecko. However this was more than a gecko – a dominant figurehead had a large crown perched on it's head. The shaft of the key was long and the teeth were a complicated cut. It was magnificent!

Sam peered into the hollow "There's a note inside." He was excited but passed it to Mala so he could further examine the golden cavity.

"What does it say?" Jet's curiosity was burning.

' *"You have solved the clue,*
*To rule number one.*
*But the path of discovery,*
*Has only just begun.*

*The key that you have,*
*Will open a cave.*
'*On Isla de Sol,*
*That the geckos have made.*

'*It's under a rock,*
'*Covered in red.*
'*At the end of the island,*
'*Blessed by the dead.*

'*It will lead to the legends,*
'*On top of a hill.*
'*In a place built by Incas,*
'*A place they live still."*

"So *Tierra Del Gecko* may still exist. First a map and now a riddle."
Jet was excited. "Do you still want to try and find it Dad?"

Sam was silent. You could see the two sides of his personality tugging
wildly. He wanted to begin the next adventure but after being stuck in
the cave with Voltar he had reassessed what was important in his life.

"I'll have to go back to Sydney first and see if your Mum wants to
come along. She has waited patiently enough for this adventurous fool,"
Sam nodded as he spoke, "but don't let me stop you three dare-devils."

Mala, Jet and Stryker looked at each other.

"I'm keen." Jet said excitedly.

"I've almost died several times with you Jet. You have made my life a
veritable living tightrope walk on the brink of destruction." Jet looked at
Stryker and realized the treacherous situations they had been through.

"Maybe it is time to quit while we are still alive," Jet commented to his colleagues.

"Are you kidding," Stryker smiled, "this may be dangerous but gee it's fun". The two geckos did a high five to solidify their friendship.

"Mala?" Jet looked at her.

"How can I possibly let you two go anywhere without my protection. If you two go, I'll have to come along," Mala smiled.

They put their front paws in the middle of a huddle.

"Well, like the three musketeers used to say – *all for one and one for all.*"

The music blared and smiles erupted at their decision. The party lasted till dawn and it went down in history as one of the greatest nights at the Bopping Beni.

# 18. The Final Days

Recovery was slow. Sam was tired, Jet's foot needed some medical attention and Stryker had a very sore back. Mala was the only one unscathed and played nurse to her weaker friends.

Over the next few days they would visit the Mercado for food, then hang out and talk in the Bopping Beni and just catch up on old news.

Sam stayed in Rurrenabaque for another week. He had rekindled the bond with his son but it was now time to leave. Sam had helped the trio as best he could in developing a plan for their next adventure. They discussed strategies and direction and they had rekindled their excitement.

Sam finally left after some very emotional tears were shed and agreed to go visit Jesca and Lucia on the way home.

Jet, Stryker and Mala stayed on in Rurre for another month and began research for their next adventure. The riddle was complicated and many enquiries and a lot of lateral thinking had to be accomplished before they set off. They also needed to develop their Spanish language and map reading skills.

The time was spent wisely, a mix of study and pleasure. Many more trips were taken to explore the Bolivian Amazon, one of the richest ecosystems in the world.

Their next adventure would be memorable, but like this one, sacrifices would need to be made. They did not know their future and they preferred it that way. The burning questions in everyones' heads were -

*Where is Isla de Sol?*
*Why is the island blessed by the dead?*
*Who are the Incas?*
The next adventure begins.
*The Gecko Tribe - Secret of the Sacred Stones.*